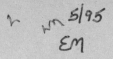

"My family will spot you for a fraud in no time flat."

"The hell they will!" Cameron retorted. "One thing I'm not, and never have been, is a fraud. I wouldn't have agreed to our bargain in the first place if I hadn't wanted to be with you."

"And why, might I ask, do you want that?" Dani scoffed.

His anger melted into something more disturbing. "Because you're the most provocative package I've ever been presented with."

"I'm *not* a package."

"Yes, you are, Dani. A package full of surprises." He moved forward and slid one arm around her waist. "The wrapping is interesting. I want to know what it's hiding."

EMMA DARCY nearly became an actress until her fiancé declared he preferred to attend the theater *with* her. She became a wife and mother. Later, she took up oil painting—unsuccessfully, she remarks. Then she tried architecture, designing the family home in New South Wales. Next came romance writing—"the hardest and most challenging of all the activities," she confesses.

Books by Emma Darcy

HARLEQUIN PRESENTS
1401—RIDE THE STORM
1433—BREAKING POINT
1447—HIGH RISK
1455—TO TAME A WILD HEART
1463—THE WEDDING
1472—THE SEDUCTION OF KEIRA
1496—THE VELVET TIGER
1511—DARK HERITAGE
1519—HEART OF THE OUTBACK

HARLEQUIN ROMANCE
2900—BLIND DATE
2941—WHIRLPOOL OF PASSION
3085—PATTERN OF DECEIT

Don't miss any of our special offers. Write to us at the following address for information on our newest releases.

Harlequin Reader Service
P.O. Box 1397, Buffalo, NY 14240
Canadian address: P.O. Box 603,
Fort Erie, Ont. L2A 5X3

EMMA DARCY

An Impossible Dream

Harlequin Books

TORONTO • NEW YORK • LONDON
AMSTERDAM • PARIS • SYDNEY • HAMBURG
STOCKHOLM • ATHENS • TOKYO • MILAN
MADRID • WARSAW • BUDAPEST • AUCKLAND

Harlequin Presents first edition March 1993
ISBN 0-373-11536-9

AN IMPOSSIBLE DREAM

CHAPTER ONE

DISASTERS COME IN THREES. The whole world knew that was a fact. Danielle Halstead knew it was fact. Therefore there could be no doubting it was a fact.

Dani brooded over this inescapable truth as she went through the motions of getting ready for the day ahead of her. She put on her baggy blue jeans and a comfortable T-shirt dyed in tones of blue and black. The colours not only suited her mood but were practical for the work she had to do. It was the kind of work guaranteed to contribute to her feeling of gloom and doom.

The first disaster had occurred eight days ago. She had hurled away her job. In more ways than one.

It wasn't her fault. She had been confronted by a situation that had simply been impossible to accept. So five years of hard work and dedication had come to an abrupt and sordid end.

Dani had made a lot of sacrifices for the sake of the career she had chosen. She loved being creative with food, and it was no mean feat to have worked her way up to the position of assistant chef in one of Sydney's most reputable restaurants. She had accepted the long night hours, accepted the fact they precluded a normal social life, accepted the loneliness forced upon her by the conditions of her job. But no way in the world could she have accepted what Julio wanted.

She had tried telling him nicely that she wasn't interested. She had tried laughing off his many and varied approaches to her. That forceful and disgusting groping in the pantry had made her burn with furious indignation, and when he had pursued her to the kitchen with more of his vile suggestions, Dani had cooled his lust at point-blank range. Her beautiful, rich, gooey, death-by-chocolate cake had met its death in a glorious splatter. All over Julio. In front of the whole kitchen staff!

That was the end. And since Julio was the boss, the parting of the ways was inevitable and irreconcilable. There was no going back.

The second disaster followed on the heels of the first. Dani's closest neighbour, Mrs. B, had sprained her ankle last weekend. Her livelihood was at risk, since she was in no condition to work. There was only one solution to the problem. Dani didn't have any work to go to. Ergo, Dani could take over Mrs. B's work until her ankle was better.

Which was why she would soon be on her way to clean Cameron McFarlane's house. The prospect did not lighten her step or her spirits. Having cleaned three houses this week as Mrs. B's stand-in, Dani was of the opinion that this work was not high on job satisfaction. She was not about to perpetuate it as an alternative career. The smell of furniture polish and toilet cleaner did not give her the same kick as the smell of a perfectly risen soufflé.

The truth of the matter was she didn't know what to do with the rest of her life. Since that awful scene with Julio, even her ambition to run her own little restaurant had curled up and died. Maybe she would get over the sense of shock and weary disillusionment in time, but right now Dani doubted it.

What she did know was that a third disaster had to be on its way, lurking in the not too distant future. Three in a row. It always happened. Dani comforted her feet by putting on her treasured Reeboks, then heaved a deep sigh and headed for the bathroom to tidy up the rest of her appearance.

The telephone rang.

Dani had no sense of premonition when she backtracked to answer it. She even smiled when she heard her mother's voice.

"I hope I didn't wake you up, dear."

Dani hadn't yet told her parents she was no longer working late hours. She hated the thought of telling them she was out of a job. And the reason. They had never approved of her choice of career in the first place. She forced a bright tone into her voice.

"No, Mum. I was up. What can I do for you?"

"It's about Christmas Day, Dani. You know it's only two weeks away. Nicole rang to say she was bringing her new man with her."

Dani grimaced. Her beautiful brilliant elder sister always had some gorgeous hunk in tow to show off her success at attracting desirable men. She never failed to make Dani feel second rate at the mating game.

"And I was wondering if you were bringing a friend home with you this year."

She had in years gone past, mostly a waiter or waitress working and travelling around Australia, and too far from family to go home for Christmas. Nicole sneeringly called them Dani's lame-duck friends. But because of what had happened with her job, Dani was out of contact with all her friends and acquaintances. Except for her neighbour, Mrs. B.

"I haven't anyone on my list at the moment," she replied. "I'll let you know in good time if I meet someone I want to bring, Mum."

"Thank you, dear. Has Nicole told you her good news?" Pride and pleasure in her voice.

Dani sighed. The perfect daughter had undoubtedly shone again. "No, we haven't been chatting lately. What's the news?"

"She's been promoted. A huge rise in salary. She says she can now afford to put a down payment on the lovely apartment where she lives. Isn't that marvellous?"

"Yes. Marvellous," Dani echoed flatly. The knowledge of what the third disaster was going to be had just thumped into her mind and heart.

Christmas Day.

Two weeks away. There was no question it would arrive dead on time, and it would undoubtedly complete the trinity of disasters.

As her mother chatted on about family affairs, Dani glumly anticipated what would happen when she went home. With her own career down the drain—impossible to keep hiding the fact forever—Nicole, the ultra-perfect daughter who never did anything wrong, would have a field day.

Like a film-clip preview, the predictable scene started playing through Dani's mind.

Daddy looking disapproving. Where was her ambition?

Nicole sweetly saying that Dani not only couldn't keep a job, she couldn't get a man and keep him, either. Of course, it was no trouble for Nicole to have both. Which she would demonstrate, right, left and centre, in prominent contrast to her feckless younger sister.

Mummy rushing in, sympathetically saying it was no good crying over spilt milk, and undoubtedly Dani would eventually do something good.

Daddy and Nicole exchanging knowing little smiles at the complete impossibility of this platitude coming true.

And so on and so on.

Utter disaster.

Dani knew perfectly well that competing with her elder sister was a totally lost cause and not worth thinking about, yet it always rankled that Nicole had been the one born under a lucky star. Not only was she bright and beautiful, but everything seemed to fall out right for her, while for Dani, the world seemed to move in the wrong direction.

She suddenly noticed the time ticking away and hurriedly ended the call from her mother. She would be late for Mrs. B's job at Cameron McFarlane's house if she didn't get a move on. And that was another thing her family wouldn't approve of.

They would never count a middle-aged cleaning woman as someone worthwhile knowing, and certainly not the best kind of friend for Dani to have.

They would be appalled that she had offered to fill in for Mrs. B. That would be called do-gooding of the worst kind. It was not Dani's responsibility. It was not Dani's problem. There was no call on her to volunteer.

For Dani it was somewhat different. She had volunteered before she ever sat down to think if it was her problem. After all, she didn't have anything better to do.

She raced into the bathroom, looked at her reflection in the mirror above the washbasin and screwed her nose up at it. Her hair was a mess. At least she never had to pay a hairdresser to get a permanent wave, Dani thought ruefully. When it came to crinkles and curls, she had an abundance of them. An overabundance. The only way to stop it from looking like a mop of frizz was to grow her hair long and keep it that way, but this morning it was an electric cloud, sticking out everywhere.

As she set about twisting the long thick mass of it into a practical plait, Dani eyed her freckles with her usual distaste. Fine skin might be fine for a country like Norway, but for the hot Australian climate, it was a curse. People said the sprinklings of freckles across her nose and cheekbones were attractive, but Dani couldn't help wishing they weren't there. She wished her skin would go a light gold in the sun. As Nicole's did.

It didn't seem fair that Nicole had inherited all the best genes. *She* had got their mother's beautiful green eyes. The least Dani could have got was her father's sherry-brown colour. But no. Hers were a mixture of the two. Hazel. The common denominator. Like her face. Which was far more round than the perfect oval that set off Nicole's beauty. And, of course, Nicole's hair was a silky honey, not plain medium brown.

Dani knew she wasn't plain, but somehow Nicole always made her feel plain. She had been told plenty of times that she had a cute, friendly face. She had a nice smile, a pert little nose, and her eyes were bright and thickly lashed. But even looking on the good side, Dani had to acknowledge she was never going to add up to *striking*. Like Nicole.

Besides which, if she attracted anyone, it invariably turned out to be the wrong sort of person. She thought of her most recent and galling experience with Julio and shuddered. Her mind instantly switched to Mrs. B. She didn't care what her family said, she liked Mrs. B and she was glad to be able to help her out at this critical time.

Nothing turned out right for Mrs. B, either. Even her name, Brwonkowskivitch, which came from having been briefly married to a Russian emigrant, was difficult to pronounce properly. Her husband had been a con man and a wastrel, and her life was one long string of disasters. Dani felt a stab of deep sympathy for her poor neighbour as she left her flat and raced upstairs to get Cameron McFarlane's house key.

Mrs. B occupied the ground-floor flat, right above Dani's basement bed-sit in the old terrace house, which was handily situated for them in the inner-city suburb of Darlinghurst. It was also cheap, which suited their pockets. Particularly in the present circumstances.

"Mrs. B?" Dani called out as she knocked on the door.

"Come on in, Dani." Mrs. B's door was unlocked and her voice came from the bedroom. "The key you need is on the end of the sideboard."

"Got it. How's the ankle this morning?"

"A lot better, thank you, Dani. I'm just getting dressed."

"Can I do anything to help?"

"No. You go on. I can manage. Say hello to dear Cameron for me."

Dani grimaced at the indulgent fondness in Mrs. B's voice. Mrs. B always described her job as 'doing for her gentlemen,' and Cameron McFarlane was her most favoured gentleman. He was a famous author, she had boasted, although Dani doubted that. She was a voracious reader, and she was completely unfamiliar with the name Cameron McFarlane. Dani suspected him of being something of a con man since Mrs. B seemed susceptible to charming liars.

"I'll do that, Mrs. B," she called out dryly.

"You'll be able to see all the books he's had published," Mrs. B said proudly. "They're in his study."

His books were about psychology or something like that, Mrs. B had told her, which was probably why Dani didn't recognise his name. "Okay. I'll have a look at them," Dani assured her. "I'll drop the key back to you when I get home and we can have a chat then."

"Have a nice day!"

"You, too. And keep off that ankle."

Dani considered psychology a murky area, fertile ground for cranks and quacks. Books on such a subject had no appeal to her. Her taste in reading ran to historical romances, science fiction and other more entertaining areas of literature.

Nevertheless, she fully intended to check on "dear Cameron's" books. As she headed outside to catch a bus to her destination, she had to concede that if "dear Cameron" lived in Double Bay, psychology must pay well. Double Bay was one of the most expensive areas in Sydney.

It was a beautiful summer morning, sparkling with summer sunshine, but Dani had too much on her mind to appreciate what a fine morning it was. She caught the appropriate bus and brooded about her life as she rode through the city.

Out of a job. No man in tow. Living in what her family considered a dump compared to Nicole's lovely apartment. No doubt about it, Christmas Day would be a disaster for her. Not too many people could be considered a complete failure at twenty-three, Dani thought with grim irony. It was a pity her family couldn't think of complete failure as a spectacular achievement.

The bus eventually came to Double Bay and Dani scrambled out at the stop Mrs. B had designated. She checked the numbers of the houses along the street, not wanting to walk past her destination. They were very up-market houses, only to be expected in this classy suburb. No failures in Double Bay.

She found the address and her eyes widened considerably at how extremely well Cameron Mc-

Farlane's brand of psychology did pay. She walked down a path, which cut through perfect lawns and tropical gardens, and led to a house that could possibly be called one of the architectural wonders of the world.

It had numerous levels and shapes in its structure, and the roof line was quite spectacular with rows of skylights radiating out from a central dome. Dani quite looked forward to exploring the interior. It was certainly the finest home of the four that she had been to this week.

The first had been Mr. Newbold's renovated terrace house at Woollhara. That had been a relatively easy job, and Dani had been quite touched by Mr. Newbold's concern over Mrs. B. He was a widower of about sixty and clearly a lonely man because he had followed Dani around, talking about Mrs. B all the time, obviously missing her company.

Mr. Clifford at Randwick and Mr. Kenway at Elizabeth Bay had both chosen to go out for the day while Dani cleaned their homes. Dani hoped that Mr. McFarlane had gone out for the day, as well. She wasn't in the mood for courteous small talk with a stranger. She could get on much faster if she had the house to herself. Following Mrs. B's instructions, Dani rang the doorbell to announce her arrival, then used the house key to let herself in.

She closed the door behind her and stood stock-still, gaping at the mind-boggling splendour and spaciousness of the foyer. It was circular, like the glass dome set into the roof some twenty feet above it, pouring light onto a pool filled with waterlilies and orchids and other exotic plants. A fountain played softly over the greenery and artfully arranged rocks and what looked like driftwood but was probably specially sculpted pieces to complement everything else.

The floor was patterned with mosaic tiles in terracotta and white. The wall was painted in the palest of terracotta pinks, and had a rich sheen that reflected the light. Four sets of double doors led off from the foyer, counting the entrance doors behind Dani. They were symmetrically spaced—right, left, front, back.

Mrs. B had told Dani to take the left-hand doors to get to the master bedroom suite at the end of the hallway. Her first job in every house was to strip the bed, collect the towels from the bathroom and get the laundry started.

The only sound she could hear was the water from the fountain, so Dani figured she had the place to herself. Otherwise Mr. McFarlane would have come to check her out after she had rung the doorbell. She had been standing here long enough for him to do so. In fact, it was time she got moving.

Her footsteps seemed to echo loudly on the tiled floor as she crossed the foyer to the left-hand doors. It made her feel like tiptoeing, but that was ridiculous. There was no-one to hear her.

The doors opened to a wide hallway, lit by a row of skylights. There were quite a few rooms leading off from the hallway, but Dani didn't bother looking into them. Time for that later. She headed straight for the master bedroom to get started on her work.

She opened the door and came to another dead halt. It was not the sight of the splendour and spaciousness of the room that caused her stillness this time. It was the sight of the naked man on the bed.

First there was the shock of finding she was not alone in the house.

Then there was the shock of the body itself.

It was sprawled out in front of her in the relaxed abandonment of sleep, and it was prime beefcake. No other description could do it justice. It could have leapt to real live flesh and blood from the centrefold of one of *those* magazines.

Dani shook her head in dazed disbelief. She simply couldn't imagine that such a body belonged to Cameron McFarlane. Mrs. B's other gentlemen were all over fifty. This body showed no sign of venerable age. Dani felt a little stab of grateful relief that it was lying front down. As it was, she had a riveting eyeful of male virility. She didn't need any further confirmation on that score.

The man was built like a world-champion swimmer: broad-shouldered, strongly muscled arms and back, slim-hipped, taut cheeky buttocks, long powerful legs. Most impressively athletic.

Dani found her eyes roving back to his bottom where a provocative strip of paler flesh interrupted the smooth tan of the rest of his body. As male bottoms went, it could certainly be classified as cute and sexy. Dani couldn't help thinking she wouldn't mind waking up in the morning to a body like that lying beside her. Of course, he would have to be more than a body for her to want that situation, but purely on an aesthetic level, he was some sight to behold.

Maybe he had a face that looked like it fell off the back of a truck, Dani thought irreverently. It was mostly buried in a pillow from her present viewpoint. His hair was thick and black and straight, cut to collar level at the back. It wasn't closely cropped to his head, so he couldn't really be a world-champion swimmer. The one visible ear was neatly shaped and tucked close to his head. Dani suspected that with so many physical assets, it was unlikely that his face didn't match the rest of him. Some people seemed to get everything.

Well, this wasn't getting the laundry done, Dani told herself. Although she couldn't see how to strip the bed with him sprawled over one sheet and the other screwed up under the lower half of his legs.

Dani considered waking him. That could be a tricky operation. What if he rolled over and stretched out as he swam up from sleep? It could be somewhat embarrassing for both of them. On the other hand, he might sleep on for hours, which would put her behind in her work.

Her eyes dropped to the quilt, which lay rumpled on the floor at the base of the bed. If she covered him with that . . . very gently . . . he would never even know she had viewed him naked. Not for sure, anyway. It seemed the best solution. Then she could wake him up without any compunction at all. She had a job to do, and if this *was* Cameron McFarlane—which still seemed most unlikely—he knew perfectly well she had a job to do.

Dani moved forward quietly. As she gathered up the fallen quilt a scrap of black lace and silk fell out. Dani dropped the quilt and picked up the tiny garment. A very sexy pair of female panties. Unless this man was a closet transvestite, there was only one conclusion to be drawn from it. The empty champagne bottle sitting in an ice bucket on one bedside table added to the evidence, and the two champagne glasses on the other bedside table confirmed it.

That certainly settled things in Dani's mind. The laundry had to be done. She even had an extra bit of it. She crumpled the small confection of silk and lace up in her hand and lifted the quilt over the dangerous lower half of lover boy's body. Then she took up a strategic position next to the bedside table.

"It's past nine o'clock," she announced in a crisp, matter-of-fact voice. "And you're messing up my work schedule."

His face burrowed farther into the pillow, indicating that her voice was an unwelcome intrusion.

"Are you Cameron McFarlane?" Dani demanded.

Maybe he was a son or a nephew. She distinctly recalled Mrs. B telling her that all her gentlemen were either widowed or had never been married. This man undoubtedly fell into the confirmed bachelor category, but that didn't prove his identity. On the other hand, what was he doing in the master bedroom if he was only visiting?

The head lifted, albeit reluctantly. Dani suspected he had a hangover from the way he squinted at her out of one eye, but she was right about the face. It more than matched the body. It could even qualify as a matinee idol face.

A wing of black hair flopped attractively over a high wide forehead. His black eyebrows had the kind of punctuated arch that was flirtatiously challenging. The eye that looked blearily at her was blue. A clear, vivid blue. His nose had a strong and rather sharp ridge line. It sat with perfect symmetry above a mouth that might have been wasted on a man, but wasn't on him. A firm, squarish jaw line was darkened by unshaven stubble, but that only added to the he-man virility he emanated. He was handsome all right, and the mature character lines on his face wiped out any plastic glossiness about his good looks. Dani figured he was probably in his early thirties.

"Who are you?" he growled at her.

"How about you answer my question first?" Dani returned reasonably.

"Of course I'm Cameron McFarlane. Who the hell else would I be?"

"How would I know? I've never seen you before in my life," Dani pointed out. "But if you're him, you ought to know who I am. You were notified that I was coming."

He winced, shook his head as though to clear it, then frowned at her. "Not Mrs. B's stand-in?" he muttered incredulously.

"Got it in one," Dani affirmed.

He rolled onto his side, propped himself up on one elbow, pried open his other eye and looked her up and down. It was a good thing she had thought of covering him up with the quilt, Dani decided. He hadn't even checked that he was decently covered. Not only that, he was doing a good job of undressing her, his eyes stripping her of her baggy jeans and T-shirt, and lingering with interest on the pertness of her full breasts.

"You don't look like a cleaning lady," he observed, lifting his gaze to hers again and offering a whimsical little smile.

Dani was not amused. This guy was obviously a dyed-in-the-wool womaniser. "You don't look like a fusty old absent-minded professor of psychology either," Dani retorted.

That surprised him. He cocked one eyebrow in disbelief. "Mrs. B told you that?"

"Not exactly," Dani admitted, her mouth quirking with irony. "I had this image of someone like Freud in my mind. And I had the impression from the indulgent way Mrs. B talks about you that you needed looking after."

His face broke into a slow grin, designed to melt any stony heart at three paces. Dimples appeared in his cheeks. "Oh, I do," he said. "And Mrs. B does it beautifully."

Oh, boy! Dani thought, ignoring the stupid flutter in her stomach. He was a charmer, all right. He undoubtedly had poor Mrs. B curled around his little finger. He probably had every woman of his acquaintance ready to jump hoops for him. Including his obliging companion of last night. Who had left him a souvenir to remember her by.

Dani unloosened the black panties from her hand and dangled them from her finger. "A pity your girlfriend isn't into housework. As it is, I guess I'm expected to do her laundry as well as yours. Which I'll get on with if you'll kindly vacate the bed.''

His grin turned into a crooked appeal. "Mrs. B usually wakes me up with a cup of coffee. And then she cooks me a proper breakfast."

Dani constructed a sympathetic look. "Well, you'll appreciate Mrs. B all the better when she's on her feet again, Mr. McFarlane. Meanwhile, you'll just have to hang tough. I'm only here to clean."

She picked up the ice bucket with the dead bottle of champagne, tucked it under her arm, then rounded the bed to collect the two dirty glasses. "I'll take these to the kitchen. When I get back, Mr. McFarlane, I want to strip the bed. I'd appreciate it if you finished with the bathroom as soon as possible, too. That's if you don't want dirty towels left lying around."

She walked briskly to the doorway, constructed a condescending smile, then turned around and bestowed it on him. "If you have a coffee maker, I'll put it on. Now that you mention it, I could do with a cup. Then when you're ready, you can pour yourself as much coffee as you like."

She sailed off down the hallway, leaving him in no doubt that she was not at his beck and call. Cleaning a house was one thing. Being a slave was quite another. Dani would never be a slave to the likes of him.

Cameron McFarlane was the male equivalent of her sister. He was obviously accustomed to everything falling into his lap when and how he wanted it. With his brand of good looks and sex appeal, he barely had to lift a finger for that to happen, and if he was brilliant, as well, life was his ball to play with.

It was positively sickening the way some people had it all. It gave Dani a lot of satisfaction to put "dear Cameron" on the loser's end today. It might only be one little pinprick to his ego, but it did her a power of good to sweep the mat out from under his feet. The bed sheets, in this case. Which was even better. The way he used Mrs. B was shameless.

On the other hand, Dani wished he might find her attractive. Of course, he wouldn't. She was too ordinary for the likes of him. But if he did... Dani's mind blossomed with the beauty of how it would be if she could take Cameron McFarlane home with her on Christmas Day.

She wouldn't be regarded as a feckless failure then. Oh, no! Her father would be most impressed that she had a famous author in tow. Her mother would be dazzled by his looks. And Nicole—Dani almost laughed out loud—Nicole would be green with envy.

An impossible dream, of course. But it was a fine fantasy.

Dani decided to develop it all day, thinking up all the mad ways of making it come true. She needed something to amuse her. Brooding over disasters was too depressing. The proposition of how to turn the third disaster into a triumphant success was much better for her mental health.

It would be even better if she could actually get Cameron McFarlane to do it.

One day out of his life. That was all she wanted. One beautiful, scintillating day that would make up for all the put-downs and disapproval she invariably suffered from some members of her family. In fact, if she didn't have her grandmother to stick up for her, as Grandma always did, Dani would be tempted not to go home at all this Christmas.

But with Cameron McFarlane in tow...

The question was... how to get his cooperation?

CHAPTER TWO

THE WAY TO A MAN'S HEART is through his stomach.
Or so her grandmother said. It had been one of the
reasons Dani had become a chef.

Experience showed getting to a man through his
stomach was not a well-proven fact. Certainly not as
well-proven as disasters in threes. Dani had never told
her grandmother this. However, she was now desperate, and since it was an old saying, she was prepared
to give it the benefit of the doubt just one more time.

If she had one superlative talent, if there was one
sure way for her to make a unique impression on anyone, cooking was it. Not even Nicole could do with
food what Dani could do with food.

Therefore, while it was somewhat galling to backtrack on cooking Cameron McFarlane a proper
breakfast, the thought of maybe getting him to come
home with her on Christmas Day made it a prime tac-
tical manoeuvre.

Apart from which, she could then get him talking
while he ate it. Communication had to be established
if she was to probe for possibilities to pounce on. And
develop. She probably didn't have a chance in hell of
capturing his interest. But what the heck! She had

nothing better to do, and it was much more interesting than doing laundry.

Dani found the utility room, tossed the black panties into the laundry tub, then opened the next door, which happily led into the kitchen. It was a beautifully equipped kitchen, designed for efficiency of movement and with great preparation space. Like the rest of the house—what she had seen of it so far—no amount of money had been spared in providing the best. Dani beamed her approval.

Having dumped the ice bucket and glasses in the sink, she examined the contents of the refrigerator. She spotted half a leg of ham, some free-range eggs and a collection of cheeses. The fruit and vegetable holders yielded up more goodies—button mushrooms, tomatoes, shallotts, oranges, mangoes. No doubt about it, she could deliver. Piece of cake!

Armed with this knowledge, Dani returned to the master bedroom. Cameron McFarlane had obligingly vacated the bed. She stripped off the sheets and pillow slips, bundled them under her arm, then headed for what had to be the door to the ensuite bathroom. She pressed her ear to it and picked up the sound of a running shower. She knocked on the door, then opened it a couple of inches so he could hear her voice.

"Hey, you in there," she called out. Best to get things on an informal basis as fast as she could, Dani decided. "Do you feel up to eating a proper breakfast?"

Silence . . . except for the running shower.

Dani pushed the door open a little farther and raised her voice. "Cameron? Can you hear me?"

"I heard you." Derisive.

"You didn't answer." Accusing from her.

"I'm contemplating what caused the sudden change of heart." A mocking drawl.

"Christmas spirit," she replied. It was more or less the truth. It certainly had something to do with Christmas, anyway.

"It came upon you with a flash of light, did it?"

"You want to stand there under the shower, psychoanalysing the spirit of Christmas, or do you want breakfast? This offer is one time only. It is not open-ended."

Pause for thought. "Can you cook?"

Got him, Dani thought. "This is your lucky day. You're talking to one of the world's leading experts."

There was a gurgling sound that could have been a scornful laugh. "Okay. You can try," he answered, and there seemed to be a thread of indulgence or smug amusement in his tone.

"Keep thinking like that, Cameron, and we are definitely *not* going to get on like a house on fire."

"I promise to eat it."

The ultimate insult! So much for trying to be attractive, Dani thought. She considered serving him up two charred pieces of toast and eggs that had been cooked to the consistency of rubber. Serve him right. Pride wouldn't allow it.

"I haven't got all day, so hurry up out of that shower. I don't like to be kept waiting," she warned. The picture of charred toast loomed invitingly. "If you do keep me waiting, it will be all the worse for you."

"I'll be there when the whips are cracking," he said, and there was no doubt about it this time. Laughter in his voice.

Dani frowned, suddenly wondering if he was into whips and kinky things like that. She had heard of such deviants. If he was, she would simply have to cross him off her list of people she could take home on Christmas Day. Which was a shame, because he was the only eligible male on it.

She shut the bathroom door loudly to punctuate her departure, then whizzed to the other end of the house. Having dumped the bed linen into the washing machine, she poured in some detergent and turned the appropriate switches. With a bit of trial and error she heard water start to run into the machine and decided she had got the switches right.

Her activity in the kitchen carried far more confidence. She put the coffee maker on, cut up some oranges and a mango and put the fruit pulp through the blender, then prepared all she needed to cook the perfect nutritional breakfast. Having completed that task, she set a place for him in the breakfast alcove adjoining the kitchen, then paused to admire the view from the window there.

A swimming pool glittered beyond a huge paved terrace. A barbecue arrangement had been built on the kitchen side. Luxurious outdoor furniture was spread out for the ultimate in convenience and comfort. Beyond the pool, the ground fell away in landscaped terraces to the harbour front.

Cameron McFarlane had a prime position, Dani thought. Quite clearly he wanted the best and went after it. Which was somewhat dampening. Dani quickly shrugged it off. Nothing ventured, nothing gained. Besides, she might not be the sexiest or most glamorous girl of his acquaintance, but she was willing to bet she was the best cook.

She went to the stove and put the pans on ready to heat. When she heard him coming she poured the fresh juice from the blender into a long glass. As he entered the kitchen, she turned to him with her best smile.

"Try this," she invited, offering him the fruit drink.

Her heart gave a little jiggle as he walked towards her. On his feet, he was certainly an imposing figure of a man—over six feet tall, Dani assessed—and the physique she had surveyed in the raw was just as impressive clothed in blue shorts and a white knit sports shirt. His cleanly shaven face looked even more handsome, and there was a nerve-steeling glint of devilment in the blue eyes. Dani had no trouble reading the intention. He was disposed to have a bit of fun with her.

"I'm sorry," he said condescendingly. "I've forgotten your name."

What a put-down! Dani instantly crossed him off her list. Too cocksure. Too arrogant by far. And no matter how stunningly gorgeous he was in the flesh, the last thing she needed at her side on Christmas day was a guy who would put her down in front of her family.

"Danielle Halstead," she answered curtly.

"Ah!" he said, as though remembering. "And people call you Dani."

"That's true."

"I didn't initially connect you to Mrs. B because I thought she was sending a male cleaner in her place." He switched on a dazzling smile. "I'm glad I was wrong."

Dani sternly told her heart to stop misbehaving so stupidly. Of course he was glad he was wrong! He was getting his breakfast cooked, wasn't he?

"Well, Dani, let's see what one of the world's leading experts can do with breakfast," he said right on cue, confirming her opinion of him.

She had been absolutely stupid to even think of backtracking on breakfast, Dani thought resentfully. The only pleasure left in it was to make him eat his condescension.

"Breakfast will be ready in ten minutes," she said dismissively, but he didn't take the hint to move away and sit down. He propped himself against the cupboards in a relaxed pose, clearly intending to enjoy watching her efforts. "How do you like your coffee?" Dani bit out.

"Black and two sugars."

She poured him a cup and shoved it along the counter towards him. "Is the fruit juice to your taste?"

"Delicious." A flicker of curiosity. "Where did Mrs. B find you?"

"I'm her neighbour."

"As in the good Samaritan?"

The light tinge of mockery caught Dani on the raw. It was the kind of thing Nicole would say, and precisely how she would say it. The idea of taking Cameron McFarlane home for Christmas was clearly a disastrous one. Nicole and he would hit it off like soul mates.

"I suppose you think I'm stupid for volunteering to help a woman who depends on her cleaning jobs to make a living?" Dani snapped.

His eyes sharpened, noting the flush on her cheeks and the bright belligerence in her eyes. "No, I don't," he said quietly.

"And I suppose you think I'm stupid for volunteering to cook your breakfast?" Dani steamed on.

He held up a hand in a trucelike gesture. "Hey, wait a bit! You're getting excited . . ."

"Don't take me for granted, Mr. McFarlane."

"Cameron?" he tried, eyebrows slanting appealingly.

"Don't take me for granted, Cameron. I'm not one of your women." She managed a sneer. "I was being nice to you. That's all."

Both hands up in appeasement. "Okay, okay. I got off on the wrong foot—"

"You certainly did."

"And I'm going to start again."

"Fine!"

"Everything forgiven?"

It confused Dani for a moment. He looked genuinely contrite. He sounded genuinely contrite. And that didn't seem to accord with the character she had given him. She swung away and took herself over to the stove to start cooking his breakfast.

"Mrs. B hasn't got any family, you know," she said by way of bridging the awkward little silence.

"I know."

She snapped on the gas-ring switches to heat up the pans, then beat the eggs with unnecessary but satisfying vigour. "You mean a lot to her. For some reason, unknown to me, she likes you."

"Maybe I've got some good points," he suggested whimsically.

She beetled him a sceptical look. "Maybe Mrs. B is a lonely old woman who likes to mother you."

"There's nothing wrong with that," he pointed out peaceably.

"No. There isn't anything wrong with that," Dani agreed grudgingly. Except he obviously took advantage of it.

"Well?" Another appeal for her goodwill.

"You know what would really give Mrs. B pleasure?" Dani fired at him.

"What?"

"If you sent her some flowers and a get-well message."

"I hadn't thought of that."

She shot him a look of appeal. "It wouldn't hurt you, would it? To make her feel...well, missed...and cared about? I know she's only your cleaning lady, but you did say she looks after you beautifully."

"You're right," he agreed good-naturedly. "What's her address?"

Dani told him and he moved straight to the wall telephone. She turned her attention to the stove and began cooking. The order of two dozen red roses brought a smile to her lips. Mrs. B would think it was a slice of heaven. A cynical little voice whispered that

Cameron McFarlane was probably well used to sending red roses, and it wouldn't really mean a thing to him. But at least he hadn't baulked at doing it, one point in his favour.

He dictated his message for the card. "Missing my favourite lady. Cameron."

What a womaniser! Quite cynical. All the same, Dani had to admit Mrs. B would love being called his favourite lady. Dani heaved a deep sigh of satisfaction. It was nice to have nice things happen to you. For someone like Mrs. B, nice things happening weren't exactly thick on the ground.

Dani popped two slices of bread into the toaster, pressed the button on the microwave to heat up the plate ready for serving, turned the omelette, checked that the tomatoes and mushrooms were nicely simmering, added a sprinkling of shallots and felt supremely content with the delicious smells drifting up to her nose.

"Am I redeemed?"

The note of hopeful appeal in his voice made her mouth twitch, despite her inner disapproval of him. She flashed him a derisive look. "That depends on your motive. Which, I suspect, would not bear too close an examination."

"I take it that breakfast is my reward," he said dryly.

The microwave pinged. The toast popped. She swiftly spread butter over the toast, removed the warm plate from the oven, arranged his breakfast on it with deft artistry, flicked off the gas switches, then turned to face him with her offering.

"It's not burnt. Sometimes it pays to be generous," she tossed at him as she carried the plate to the alcove.

He followed, sniffing appreciatively. "Smells great. Looks great..."

"I happen to be—"

"Yes, I know." He grinned at her as he sat down. "One of the world's leading experts. I shall not doubt your word again. New start. Right?"

Dani allowed herself to feel somewhat mollified even though his charm was the ultimate in slick. "Right," she agreed, wondering if she could risk putting him back on the list.

He was open to suggestion. He was good at pretending an interest. He had dropped that off-putting arrogance. The question was... how to make it worth his while to do what she wanted of him? After all, he probably had his own family to go to on Christmas Day. On the other hand, Cameron McFarlane did not impress her as a committed family person.

"Why do I get the feeling that you're measuring me up for another strike?" he inquired.

Those twinkling blue eyes really were dynamite, Dani thought. "Eat," she commanded, and left him to do so while she cleaned up in the kitchen and thought some more.

If she could get him to turn in the right kind of performance, he would certainly do the trick of sidetracking her family from asking all the burning questions Dani didn't want to answer. But first she had to capture his interest, and not just play interest. He had read her correctly. She did need to strike him, somehow...

"This is a superb omelette," he said.

Back to cooking, Dani thought. Perhaps her grandmother *was* right. If she made him a very special lunch to top off the breakfast, and started being really nice to him...

"I'm glad you're enjoying it," she said, beaming him a bright smile.

"Why don't you have a coffee break and come and join me at the table?" he invited. His eyes merrily teased her as he added, "In the spirit of Christmas, peace and goodwill."

The perfect opening. "Thank you," Dani said with real gratitude. "I'm about ready for a cup. Want a refill on yours?" she added, demonstrating her goodwill.

"Please."

She provided them both with coffee and then sat down opposite him. He was making short work of his breakfast, eating with relish. So he ought, Dani thought smugly. He wouldn't get a perfectly cooked breakfast like that every day.

"Do you have a family you go to for Christmas?" she asked.

The pleasure on his face seemed to click out, leaving it oddly expressionless. His eyes lost their sparkle. "No family," he said with forced lightness.

"I'm sorry," Dani said automatically, sensing an aloneness that she had not associated with him before. Although she sometimes wished to be free of ties of obligation, she would never wish to be completely cut off, on her own.

His lips stretched into a sardonic little smile. "No need to be. I do quite well by myself. What about you? A large family?"

Dani sighed. "Not so much large as heavy."

He looked quizzical. "A *heavy* family?"

"There are always expectations to live up to," Dani answered dryly.

His face broke into a grin, sunshine emerging from a cloud. "Like becoming one of the world's experts at cooking?"

"Something like that." It was far too soon to outline her problems. She had to check out the possibilities first. "So what do you do with yourself on Christmas Day?" she asked.

He shrugged. "There are always invitations I can take up if I want to."

Naturally, Dani thought. A man like him would be welcomed by a lot of people, particularly women. "Anything special this year?" she probed.

He shook his head. "I'll probably spend a quiet day here. I'll be flying out to the United States early on Boxing Day."

At least she had the all-clear. He was free to accompany her home, if she could get him to cooperate. That was a big if. Dani tried to rally her confidence. It was a pity she wasn't any good at flirting. Nicole was so expert at it that Dani had automatically declined to bother with such an art.

Cameron McFarlane cleaned his plate with a piece of toast, then sat back with an air of complete satisfaction. He gave her a twinkling look of approval that had her toes curling. "How did you learn to cook like that?"

"With a great deal of application," Dani answered with a self-derisive laugh. Stick to cooking, my girl, she told herself. It was her best bet for softening him up to see things her way.

The telephone rang and Cameron pushed his chair back to get to his feet. Dani started to rise also, figuring she had better get to the cleaning if she was going to take time off to concoct a seductive lunch.

"Stay. Finish your coffee," he urged.

"It's finished. And I've got work to do."

He grimaced at her argument as he moved to answer the telephone. Dani picked up his breakfast things and took them to the sink. She heard his end of the brief conversation while she stacked the dishwasher. He didn't sound too happy with what was being said by the other party on the line. In fact, when he hung up the telephone, he gave vent to some colourful curses.

"Something wrong?" Dani asked sympathetically.

He rolled his eyes. "I can't believe it! The man burst into tears on me. A grown man..."

"There must have been a reason."

Frustration edged his voice. "No reason at all. I hired these people to cater a party tomorrow night. They're supposed to be the best. Gourmet food. Reliable quality. Perfect service..."

"Peregrine and Sylvester."

"Yes." He looked startled at her knowledge.

"And that was Peregrine to say he couldn't possibly cope." It was a statement from her, not a question.

Cameron nodded.

"And when you remonstrated, he broke into hysterical sobs." Another statement.

"How on earth could you know that?"

"Elementary. Peregrine and Sylvester specialise in high-tone parties."

Cameron looked bewildered. "So?"

He obviously needed more explanation. Dani patiently gave it to him. "It's a wonder Peregrine thought to call and cancel at all. About ten days ago he attempted suicide in a very half-hearted way. Quarter-hearted is probably more accurate."

"Whatever for?"

"Because Sylvester was lured away by another lover. It was only a temperamental suicide, of course, to blackmail Sylvester into coming back, but I'm afraid it didn't work. The faithless Sylvester has flown off to Venice. The word in the trade is that he's been promised a luxury train trip on the Orient Express as well as fun and games amongst the gondoliers."

"My God! How did you find all this out?"

"Gossip. Everyone gossips like mad in the trade." She gave him a wise look to punctuate the point in case he was slow to catch on.

He winced.

Dani decided some defence of her profession was in order. "Peregrine and Sylvester are usually very professional in their work, but they do have their little emotional traumas now and then. Sylvester will eventually come back. I'm told he always does. Then things will go straight back to normal."

"What about my party?" Cameron complained.

"You could postpone it for about six months," Dani offered helpfully. "By then . . ."

"What connection do you have to the catering business, Dani?" Cameron asked curiously.

"I've been working as a chef for years. For the past twelve months I've been assistant chef at Julio's Restaurant," she added with considerable pride. The fact that she was no longer there wasn't relevant.

His face cleared of all puzzlement. It was as though a light had been switched on behind his eyes. They turned to an incandescent blue. "A chef. A trained chef." His mouth widened into a distinctly wolfish grin. "What are you doing tomorrow night, Dani?"

A thousand-watt light globe suddenly clicked on in Dani's mind. The gold specks in her hazel eyes gleamed very brightly. "Expensive," she said. "Very expensive."

It did not deter him one bit. He leapt at the bait with teeth still bared. "How much would it cost me to lure you into catering my party?" Bribery and corruption obviously no object.

"Well, Cameron," she said with a lilt. "I can see you'd be socially embarrassed if you couldn't feed your guests the way you want to. And since I have a very fine understanding of social embarrassment, maybe...just maybe...we can ywork something out. Come to an understanding, so to speak."

He looked at her warily. "You would consider doing it? You can get out of your job at Julio's?"

She wasn't about to admit she was already out. When it came to bargaining, Dani was no dumb chick. "I can, with some considerable effort, make myself free tomorrow night," she said slowly. Then in a dubious tone, "How big is the party?"

"Small," he encouraged. "Only about twenty people."

"Piece of cake." She wanted him encouraged, too. "You'll do it for me, then?"

"Maybe. I could do something really special."

"Wonderful."

"No quibbles about the cost of gourmet delicacies?"

"Spend whatever you need to."

"And then there's my time and trouble and expertise..."

"How much do you want?"

"Nothing. Nothing at all. It's not a question of money for me..."

"What do you want, then?" Frustration.

Dani smiled. She couldn't stop the smile from widening into a grin of calculating triumph. "I'll swap you..."

"Yes?"

"This party, if I can have..."

"Yes, yes?" he pumped eagerly.

"*You*—body and soul—on Christmas Day!"

CHAPTER THREE

DON'T COUNT YOUR CHICKENS before they hatch. That was always Grandma's advice. Yet Dani couldn't help feeling elated. As she made her way home, she severely cautioned herself that there was many a slip 'twixt the cup and the lip. But she was driving one of Cameron McFarlane's cars!

Despite all her commonsense attempts, it was proving impossible to bring herself down to earth. Bursts of glee kept bubbling through her. She had actually done it! Pulled off the impossible dream!

While Christmas Day had not yet come and gone, Cameron McFarlane had given his word that he would play his part. Dani had no doubt he could do it. Glorious scenes of the impact he would undoubtedly make on her family zipped in and out of her imagination. The scenes with Nicole were especially satisfying.

Success was very sweet, Dani thought exultantly. She hadn't precisely got to Cameron's heart by way of his stomach, but what she had achieved through her cooking was more than she had expected, so life was definitely looking up. Luck—in the form of Peregrine and Sylvester's dereliction of duty—had been on her side. She had every right to feel happy and high-spirited.

Dani laughed as she remembered Cameron's initial reaction to her proposition—totally stunned surprise. Then as she had explained more, his expression gradually changed to whimsical amusement. He declared it would be his pleasure to be at her side on Christmas Day, and fulfilling his role would be a piece of cake. Which was very sporting of him, considering the way she had gone about it.

He had also been rather sporting earlier when he had sent the flowers to Mrs. B. And she had really enjoyed planning the party with him. She couldn't have asked for a more cooperative partner. He had agreed to the shopping list she had made out, and lent her the car so she could get about more freely. Generous as well as sporting, Dani thought warmly. On the other hand, it must have been perfectly plain to him that there was a lot for her to do if she was to deliver what he wanted.

It was in his own interest, she reminded herself. Yet he could have left all the party work to her once the bargain had been struck between them. Instead of which, he had readily accepted the argument that there was only one of her, not two like Peregrine and Sylvester. He had followed her around the house while she cleaned, Dani delegating little jobs for him to do while he asked what she intended to serve and discussed how best it could be organised.

There had been other, more personal questions, as well. Dani had sparred with him over those, not prepared to give too much of herself away. What they had was a business agreement. Pure and simple. As it was, she found Cameron McFarlane too attractive for her own good. There was no sense in letting herself be charmed into weaving fantasies about him that couldn't come true.

Although she had got him for Christmas Day!

Dani was able to park right outside the terrace house where she lived. Not many people owned cars in this street, and certainly not a luxury model like a BMW. She hoped it would be safe overnight. Darlinghurst was not the most salubrious of suburbs, but Dani's immediate neighbourhood was relatively quiet and respectable.

She quickly carried this afternoon's purchases down to her bed-sit, then raced up the stairs to see Mrs. B.

"It's Dani," she called out from the communal hallway.

"I'm in the sitting room, Dani," came the reply.

The front room of the ground floor was Mrs. B's bedroom. It was sealed off from the hallway because of the staircase that continued up to the top-floor flat. This was occupied by a couple whose marital conflicts could be heard on all levels, and a fair way up the street, leaving Dani and Mrs. B to wonder how and why they could bear living together.

The ground-floor hallway ran straight through the house to the laundry they all shared, but the door halfway along it opened into Mrs. B's sitting room, and it was slightly ajar so that Mrs. B could listen to any comings or goings. Even the fighting couple upstairs were company for her . . . of a sort.

Dani heard *Wheel of Fortune* click off as she reached the door. "You don't have to stop watching TV, Mrs. B."

Since it served for most living purposes, the room was cluttered with furniture. Mrs. B sat in her favourite armchair, resting her injured ankle on a footstool. The remote control for the television set was poised in her hand, but it was instantly clear that she had no further interest in watching the program. Her brown eyes glowed with pleasure, giving her rather homely face a lively attraction.

"Oh, Dani! You'll never guess. I've had the most wonderful day," she enthused.

Dani spotted the red roses on the dining table out of the corner of her eye, but she didn't let on that she'd seen them. "Has the swelling in your ankle gone down?" she asked brightly.

"Almost." Mrs. B waved a dismissive hand. "I had a visitor. Henry Newbold. You know, from the Woollhara house I clean on Mondays."

Dani didn't have to act her surprise. She had been expecting to hear something else. But she easily recollected the widower who had been so concerned about Mrs. B. "That was nice of him," she said.

"Yes. And he brought me a box of chocolates and stayed a while to chat." Mrs. B was quite pink-cheeked about it. "He asked if he could call me Hilda."

Dani raised her eyebrows. A romance in the offing? She smiled as she mentally paired them together, Mr. Newbold's stiffly upright military bearing and dignified white mane of hair, Mrs. B's somewhat roly-poly build and the dyed red-grey hair permanently waved with a vengeance. However oddly matched they seemed, opposites did attract, Dani reminded herself.

Even if it was only an easing of mutual loneliness, it was something.

"He did seem to miss you a lot on Monday," Dani encouraged.

"Yes. He told me. And he seemed quite put out when the roses arrived."

"Ah!" said Dani, turning her head to acknowledge the splendid arrangement of perfect blooms. Maybe it hadn't been such a good idea after all.

"Quite put out," Mrs. B repeated with satisfaction. "Dear Cameron sent them."

"He told me he was going to," Dani affirmed, keeping her role in the affair undercover.

"I had to explain to Henry that Cameron was one of my gentlemen. Quite a young man, and like a son to me. Henry said he understood that anyone would like to have me as a mother." Her ample bosom rose and fell in deep pleasure.

Dani smothered a sigh of relief. The gesture had obviously worked out even better than she had anticipated. "Well, Cameron certainly speaks very fondly of you," she said, happy that Mrs. B felt so happy.

"A dear boy. A very dear boy, thinking of me like that."

Dani didn't think that Cameron McFarlane could properly be called a boy, but she held her tongue. "Here's your share of today's wages," she said, stepping over to the sideboard and tucking the notes into the handbag that sat there.

"I don't like taking that money from you, Dani," Mrs. B protested. "You're doing all the work."

"Half and half. We agreed, Mrs. B. I wouldn't have any work at all but for you." She grinned. "And because of you, I've got a job for tomorrow night." She explained about Cameron's party and the caterers cancelling at such impossibly short notice, but she kept the bargain they'd struck to herself. "So it's good news all around," she finished with a smile.

"That's wonderful, dear! I'm sure you'll manage very well."

"I need to get a few things done tonight, Mrs. B, so I won't stay. Are you all right for everything? Anything I can get you?"

"Don't worry about me, Dani. I can manage quite well now."

She looked as though ten years had been taken off her age. It was amazing how a few little lifts in life could make so much difference. Dani was well aware of the bounce in her own step as she went downstairs.

Her mind hummed with plans while she took a refreshing shower. First she would make her death-by-chocolate cake. While that was in the oven, she would whip up the avocado dip and start on the crepes. It was so good to feel a sense of purpose. She wanted to show Cameron McFarlane that he was getting an excellent bargain. Really impress him.

The thought came to her that she didn't have to wear her whites on this job. It was quite different to being a chef in a restaurant. She could dress up. After all, she would be mingling among the party guests as she served them, and it was better if she didn't stand out like a sore thumb.

She could wear her little black dress. It was discreet. It was also the most feminine thing she owned. Dani baulked at calling it sexy. She was *not* Nicole. She was *not* trying to compete for Cameron McFarlane's interest. *His* kind of woman would undoubtedly be a knockout, and Dani did not delude herself into thinking she could belong in that category. Not even with all flags flying. However, she could... well, try.

She wanted to look her best. That was reasonable. And she didn't want to look too much out of place. It was an opportunity to show Cameron he wouldn't be accompanying a complete frump on Christmas Day.

Dani towelled herself dry, slipped on some fresh clothes, then headed for the kitchen where she had dumped all the shopping bags. She was in the middle of lining up the ingredients for the cake when the telephone rang. A glance at the oven clock showed 6:25. Frowning over who might be calling her at this hour, she hurried to answer the summons.

"Well, I finally got you." Nicole's voice.

Dani sighed. Probably ringing up to gloat. It was never for a nice sisterly chat. "Mum told me about your promotion. Congratulations, Nicole," she slid in before the gloating got into full stride.

"Oh!" Disappointment. "Well, I've been trying to reach you all day. When I couldn't get you at home, I rang Julio's. You could have warned me you'd lost your job." Accusing.

The fat was in the fire! Dani gritted her teeth. "I didn't *lose* my job, Nicole. I walked out."

"What on earth for? You won't get a better position than you had at Julio's."

"It wasn't healthy for my social life."

A short disbelieving silence. "And that's more important to you than a career?" Absolute scorn.

"I'm evaluating my priorities," Dani said loftily.

A snort. "How's your bank balance, Dani?"

"How's yours?"

"*My* bank balance is not in question since I have the good sense to know how to forge ahead in my career. I'm merely asking about your finances because Christmas is coming up. You obviously need guidance on buying presents. I don't know what you thought you were doing last year—"

"They were fun gifts, Nicole. Haven't you ever heard of fun?" Dani interposed.

"Useless rubbish." Contemptuous dismissal. "As it happens, I saw a marvellous gift you can buy Mum . . ."

Dani seethed while Nicole described the marvellous gift. She had been suffering this kind of put-down all her life from Nicole, as though she couldn't be trusted to choose anything good, as though she had no taste at all in anything. Except food. Which didn't count with Nicole because she was always dieting.

Besides, the gifts she had brought last year had given everyone a laugh. Everyone except Nicole. No sense of humour at all. At least, not where Dani was concerned. She hadn't even raised a smile at her gift. Just rolled her eyes and turned up her nose as though it was a bad smell. Dani had bought her expensive

Lancôme soap this year, so she could wash the bad smells away. Nicole wouldn't turn up her nose at that.

"If you don't have enough money, I could go out of my way and lend you some. For a short time. Until you regain your senses," Nicole finished with typical condescension.

"Thank you for the thought, Nicole," Dani said with tightly held restraint, "but I've already bought Mum's Christmas present. And everyone else's."

A frustrated sigh. "I suppose you were out looking for another job today."

"No. I was with the latest man in my life."

"What?"

"You heard me, Nicole. Man, as in m-a-n."

"Another lame-duck boyfriend?" It was an out-and-out sneer.

Dani suffered a sudden rush of blood to the head. She was sick to death of this sniping from her oh, so superior sister. For once in her life she had a big gun up her sleeve, and the temptation to roll it out and fire it was overwhelming. It wasn't every day she could play one-upmanship with her elder sister. Christmas Day would be the big pay-off, but this was certainly a timely little bonus.

"Oh, I wouldn't call Cameron McFarlane a boy, Nicole. Not even a friend. He's a man."

"Who? What name did you say?"

"Cameron. Cameron McFarlane. He's a famous author. While I haven't asked his exact age, he certainly doesn't look like a boy. He doesn't act like a boy. He doesn't feel like a boy. I'd say he was definitely all man." So cop that, Nicole, Dani added to herself.

"You don't mean you've let yourself get involved with *him?*" Nicole answered her.

"Oh? You know Cameron, do you?"

"Of course I do. God almighty! Why do you always have to be a silly naive little fool?"

Dani came off her high with a thump. Anger stirred. "I hope you have a good reason for saying that, Nicole."

"You want to join the queue? Be a chapter in his next book? Why, do you suppose, he's interested in someone like you?"

"He happens to like me," Dani grated.

"Sure!" Nicole scoffed. "An ignorant little virgin. As foolish as they come."

"I'm not!" Dani cut in hotly.

"He'll string you along and seduce you..."

"What's it to you, Nicole? You've been gallivanting through men's bedrooms for years. You're living openly with a man right now. You're not prepared to marry him. So why hassle me and my choices? Maybe I want to be seduced."

Silence. Then, grimly, "He'll use you for his own purpose, and that will be the end of it. He's a notorious womaniser. I thought you'd have a bit more pride than that, Dani."

"And what makes you such an authority on Cameron McFarlane?" Dani challenged fiercely.

"My PR firm handles his publicity in Australia. His latest book, *The Psychology of Sex,* is currently top of the best-seller list. Been there for ten weeks. He's just finished a term of guest lectureship at Sydney University. His next book is to be called *The Psychology of Sexual Experience in the Modern Woman.*"

Hell! Dani thought. What had she got herself into? No wonder his brand of psychology paid well. Nothing like sex to sell a lot of books. And no doubt he was a first-hand authority on the subject. But that really had nothing to do with her and the bargain she had made with him. Nevertheless, she couldn't let Nicole know that.

"Which all makes him a fascinating man," she said as blithely as she could.

"Dani, I know him. You are mincemeat to him. Believe me. Get out before you're badly hurt."

"How well do you know him?" Dani demanded, refusing to budge. Nicole was obviously green with jealousy that a man like Cameron McFarlane was paying her ineffectual little sister any attention at all.

"Intimately."

A chill spread through Dani's veins. The glorious vista of triumph on Christmas Day wavered before her eyes, threatening to disintegrate. "Are you telling me that you've had sex with Cameron McFarlane, Nicole?" she demanded flatly.

"Don't be so crude, Dani."

"I'm not crude, Nicole. I'm honest. Isn't that why I'm such a cross for you to bear? Because I'm not smart and polished and sophisticated like you?" she went on, hating—absolutely hating—the idea that Cameron had bedded her sister. Unfortunately it was all too believable.

"I have tried to help you—"

"I don't want your help! I want the unadulterated truth. Have you, or have you not, been where you told me not to go?"

There was a long pregnant pause. An exasperated sigh. "You make such stupid choices, Dani—"

"Yes or no?"

"I'm only trying to protect you—"

"Yes or no?"

"He's a high-flyer—"

"Yes or no?"

"Yes!"

"Thank you."

Dani crashed the telephone receiver down in a mountainous rage against the stinking rotten fate that had led her to Cameron McFarlane and the hope that she could be a winner for once. She should have known it was too good to be true. When had she ever been a winner against Nicole? Never!

She hugged her chest to hold the pain of it in and tramped up and down the small room to work off the volatile energy charging through her. This was what came of counting chickens before they hatched. A rotten egg right in the midst of her nest of beautiful dreams.

Damn Cameron McFarlane and his careless womanising! He was no better than a rooster in a henhouse. And Nicole, of course, would have been right up his alley. Two of a kind. Sharing the highest perch above all other lesser mortals.

What a fool she had been to think that anything with a man like him could work out right for her! Dear God! Those black silk and lace panties could have been Nicole's. The thought of his naked body in intimacy with her sister's . . .

It was sickening.

Even worse was the thought of how it would have been if she'd taken him home with her on Christmas Day with Nicole knowing . . .

Sick, sick, sick.

At least she had been spared that dreadful humiliation. But now Nicole could preach about her unwise involvement with Cameron, and the loss of her job, and Christmas Day was going to be hell! So much for averting the third disaster! She had compounded it a hundredfold!

On top of everything else, she still had to do Cameron McFarlane's party with no reward for all her labour. Just because she had to reject his side of the agreement, it was no excuse to ignore her side. She had already spent a sizeable chunk of his money, and there was his car parked outside, and he was depending on her to keep her word. She had no choice but to deliver on tomorrow night's party. Her sense of integrity, her sense of professionalism, would not allow her to do anything else.

But she wouldn't bother with her little black dress. If Cameron McFarlane didn't approve of her chef's whites, too bad! Expertise was expertise, and he could jolly well be grateful for what he got. All she was going to get was a big fat zero.

Dani trudged out to the kitchen. There was work to be done and she might as well get on with it, but there was no joy in it. No joy at all. She was face to face with the undeniable, unpalatable, unchangeable truth. There was simply no escaping the fact that disasters came in threes.

CHAPTER FOUR

THE BEST LAID SCHEMES o' mice an' men gang aft a-gley.

A good word, *gang,* Dani thought glumly. Everything always seemed to gang up against her. It was a wonder Cameron McFarlane's BMW was still in the street this morning. No-one had crashed into it, either. That was probably because it was part of *his* scheme. Only *her* schemes got shot to ribbons. And it wasn't going to be much fun telling him that she had changed her mind about Christmas Day.

She brought the car to a halt in Cameron McFarlane's driveway and sat staring blankly at the closed garage doors, mentally gearing herself to face the inevitable. Cameron would want to know why she had changed her mind. Pride insisted that she not tell him it was because he had bedded her sister.

No doubt he would be only too ready to accept any reason. After all, she had pressured him into it. What possible pleasure could there be for him in spending Christmas Day at her side? Much as it pained Dani to acknowledge it, Nicole could very well be right. She probably was a silly naive little fool.

The garage door in front of her tilted open. Then the man himself was there, smiling at her, looking bare and bronzed and stunningly physical. He was wearing luminous red swim shorts. That was all. And the shorts were briefer than brief. However spectacular the red was, it did not compare with the rest of the spectacle on show.

Dani's heart contracted. *Man* was right. But he was also a man who had intimately shared all that compelling maleness with her sister. Which put him absolutely off-limits as far as Dani was concerned.

He waved her forward. Dani started the car and drove into the garage, telling herself she was here to do a job and that was all she was here for. She had to wipe her mind of everything else concerning Cameron McFarlane.

He opened her door as she switched off the engine. "More convenient for unloading in here." His voice was warmly welcoming. His smile was heart-stopping at close quarters. The twinkling blue eyes aided and abetted its striking power. "I had a feeling you'd be meticulously punctual. It's right on the dot of one o'clock."

"I keep my word." It came out sharply. Dani was more on edge than she wanted to be. She fiercely wished she didn't find him so attractive. It wasn't fair.

"So do I," he assured her, as though picking up the doubt in her mind.

Dani heaved a rueful sigh. It would have been easier for her if he'd turned out to be an absolute rotter, but she had the suspicion that somehow she intrigued him, and he would have played his part to the hilt on Christmas Day. In a way she was glad about that. It showed that her judgement wasn't always wrong. But it didn't help the situation.

She swung her legs out of the car and stood up, lifting her gaze to his reluctantly. She caught him in the act of giving her the once-over. Couldn't help himself, Dani decided cynically. An automatic reaction to the proximity of a woman. Not that he would get much satisfaction out of her. She was not dressed to show off her femininity. She was dressed for work.

The white Reeboks on her feet were the most practical shoes for her profession, expensive but well worth the money in terms of comfort since she was on her feet all the time. Her sage-green shorts—it was a very hot day—were baggy and almost knee-length. Her lemon and white top was loose enough to let the air circulate between the fabric and her skin. Her face was undoubtedly shiny from the heat since she hadn't bothered with make-up, and she had woven her thick, unruly hair into a plait from the top of her head to the nape of her neck.

It surprised her when his gaze flicked up to hers and she saw a gleam of approval—pleasure?—dancing in the blue eyes. And the smile had grown broader. It cracked her defences wide open. For some perverse reason he liked her precisely the way she was. She could feel it. But it was no good feeling it. She steeled herself against the fluttery vulnerability he evoked in her and handed him the car keys.

"There's some stuff in the trunk to be carried in, if you wouldn't mind," she said flatly.

The smile didn't falter, but one eyebrow was slightly raised. Probably psychoanalysing me, Dani thought.

Which wouldn't get him very far with her. She had a built-in resistance platform—namely Nicole—that he would never get past, no matter how clever and likeable he was.

"You sound tired, Dani. Is this going to be too much for you?"

Pride in her own abilities came to the fore and made up her mind as to her course of action. She wanted no distraction from producing her best. "Piece of cake," she said, "but business before pleasure."

He could take that any way he liked because Dani knew what she meant. She would do the job first. Then she would tell him she didn't need him any more. Not for Christmas Day or anything else. No need to go into details. Then he could get about his business, and she could get about hers. Which, at this point in time, was non-existent except for Mrs. B's cleaning. The sprained ankle would certainly be better by next Friday, so Dani wouldn't have to see Cameron McFarlane again after tonight.

There was a moment of consideration from him. "Right," he agreed. "Tell me what you want me to do."

Which was generous of him. And immediately changed the nature of the relationship between them. There was none of the casual bantering he had gone on with yesterday. She was the professional, and without knowing it, Dani exuded a self-confidence, a knowledge of her powers, a high degree of practical efficiency in her every word and action. She was in charge, and he subtly acknowledged it, doing her bidding without any argument, standing back and watching her in an admiring way if there was nothing he could do to help her.

It was a companionable afternoon. If only Nicole hadn't spoilt everything with her revelation, it would have been a very pleasurable afternoon. As it was, Dani had to continually put clamps on her responses to Cameron's almost-naked nearness and his obliging good nature.

She was also conscious of some private assessment of her going on in his mind. Perhaps she was only imagining it. Perhaps it was because she now knew what he wrote about—what he was famous for—that she kept thinking he was viewing her as an interesting subject. Whatever... She was disturbingly aware of his presence and found it increasingly difficult to keep her guard up against the compelling charisma of the man.

It was a relief when all the preparation was done and she could get away from him for a while. Cameron had offered her one of the guest bedroom suites to shower and change and generally refresh herself before the party.

Dani had little to do in regard to her appearance. Her hair was fixed in the neat plait. She had quite deliberately brought no make-up with her to punctuate the point that she was rejecting every intention of trying to look attractive for Cameron McFarlane. However, she did linger in the shower, needing to wash away the tension that somehow had her feeling all her nerves were as taut as piano wires, ready to twang at any provocation.

She pulled on her white slacks and was doing up the side buttons of the white tunic when a dreadful thought struck her. What if Nicole was invited to this party? Dani closed her eyes and shuddered. She should have brought the little black dress to wear. She should have...

No! Cold hard reason asserted that whatever had gone on between Cameron and Nicole was over. Past history. And the way Nicole had spoken about him meant that Cameron had dumped her, not the other way around. Therefore, Nicole's pride wouldn't allow her to be here even if she had been invited. Dani breathed freely again. The humiliation of being seen by her sister as Cameron's cook instead of his girlfriend was not about to be heaped on her head.

Six more hours should see the mess through, Dani consoled herself. She squared her shoulders and set off to do a last-minute check of everything. The guests were supposed to start arriving at eight o'clock. She had twenty minutes' grace to ensure that nothing had been forgotten.

The set of double doors opposite the entrance to the foyer opened to a living room, which to Dani was the acme of casual elegance. The tiled floor, which continued from the fabulous fountain foyer, was broken by squares of geometrically patterned carpet. Around these were grouped leather lounges and armchairs, serviced by low granite tables. Brass sculptures were mixed with indoor ferns and palms. A magnificently provisioned bar ran along one wall, with a brass foot rail and leather and brass bar stools. The wall facing the outside patio and swimming pool was all glass, with sliding doors that readily expanded the huge entertainment area. For the kind of informal party planned for tonight, it was absolutely ideal.

Cameron was behind the bar, filling ice buckets and planting bottles of champagne in them. "Have a drink with me before the madhouse begins," he invited. "You've more than earned a few minutes' relaxation, Dani."

She hesitated, reluctant to ease the barrier she had drawn between them. Yet it seemed churlish to refuse. "All right."

She was conscious of his eyes flicking over her chef's uniform as she walked to the bar. She half-expected a comment on it, but none came. She had the impression he was totting another configuration up in his brain, and he didn't particularly like the answer it was pointing to. She slid onto a bar stool, trying not to notice how well his white trousers fitted him, nor how the navy blue shirt seemed to deepen the colour of his eyes.

Before Dani realised what he was doing, there was a loud pop, and he was pouring champagne into two glasses. "I didn't mean you to open a bottle just for me. A soft drink . . ." His smile choked off the rest of her protest.

"I thought it was time for us to drink a toast."

"A toast to what?"

"Our partnership." He handed her a glass and clinked it with his.

"Short and sweet," she muttered, then sipped cautiously at the wine. It was very nice but she couldn't afford to let anything go to her head.

"Will they be missing you at Julio's tonight?" Cameron asked.

"No."

"Have any difficulty getting the time off?"

"No."

"They can do without you?"

Dani shrugged. "They have to. I don't work there any more."

He frowned. "I thought you said . . ."

"I did work there until a week ago." She gave him an ironic little smile. "It was easy to make myself free for you. I've now joined the army of the unemployed."

"Why?" Curious rather than critical.

Her smile became more crooked. "We had a difference of opinion about something."

She took another sip of wine. Throughout her time at Julio's she had tasted the odd glass of good wine from the unfinished bottles left behind by customers. This champagne was very good. Creamy was the way the experts described it.

"You're a woman of very strong opinions," Cameron remarked, more of a question than a statement, his eyes teasing and probing at the same time.

"No, I'm not. I have a very open mind." So much for his psychoanalysis, Dani thought. Her eyes flashed a warning. "What I do have is a strong sense of where I'm going and what's right and wrong for me."

His mouth quirked. "I stand corrected . . . again."

"I'd give it up if I were you."

"And if I don't?"

"You might learn something you don't want to learn."

He laughed. "You can put me into a neatly labelled pigeonhole, but I can't do that to you?"

"That's about the size of it," Dani returned loftily.

His grin held an appreciative warmth that tingled right down to Dani's toes. "I must admit you are proving to be a challenge. Rather unique... amongst the women of my acquaintance."

"Of which there are undoubtedly many," Dani snapped, trying desperately to reline her defences and squash her vulnerability to his undermining charm.

She had to get his mind off her. She didn't need to have him burrowing under her skin. Dani frantically searched for a way to divert his attention away from herself. Then a flash of inspiration hit.

"In fact," she said brightly, "I've been wondering what's wrong with you. Now I know."

One eyebrow rose. "Does something have to be wrong?"

"Oh, yes. Quite definitely yes."

"Why?"

"Because you're not married. That's unnatural. You haven't got a lack of choice," Dani pointed out reasonably. "And you're thirty-something years of age without having achieved a permanent relationship with a woman you can live with. Which leaves two alternatives as I see it."

"Which are?" He looked amused.

"You're either inordinately fussy, and horribly self-centred. Or..."

"Or?"

"You're not really interested in women at all."

"What?" That wiped the amusement off his face.

"It's a theory," Dani went on matter-of-factly. "What's a man trying to prove when he keeps fluttering from woman to woman? Doesn't that suggest that something is wrong with him? That maybe he's not sure of his sexuality?" There, take that, she thought. A little bit of psychoanalysis from Dani Halstead.

"Maybe he simply hasn't found what he's looking for," Cameron muttered.

"Maybe the fault lies within himself," Dani countered, then shrugged with a sublime air of indifference. "But whatever the cause, it's none of my business."

The door chimes sounded.

Dani grinned at him. "Action stations!" She slid off the stool to head for the kitchen. "Have a good party, Cameron," she tossed over her shoulder. "Maybe you'll find what you're looking for tonight."

He muttered something she didn't catch. Dani was laughing to herself. She had set him back on his heels, good and proper. Taught him a lesson. She figured Cameron McFarlane could do with quite a few lessons. He was far too smug about his own powers. She propped herself against the kitchen cupboards, sipping happily at the glass of champagne until it was time to start the first round of hors d'oeuvres. An hour later the party was really humming. People were floating on champagne as though there was no tomorrow. "Are you celebrating something?" Dani asked Cameron when he carried an empty tray out to the kitchen.

"Ten weeks on the *New York Times* best-seller list," he affirmed. "Got any more of those little crepe things with the lobster and mango fillings? Or the spinach and cheese?" he added hopefully. "They went like hot cakes."

"About ready to come out of the oven. I'll bring them in." She flashed him an accusing look. "You said about twenty guests. I did a head count of twenty-eight."

An apologetic grimace. "People bring people. I'm afraid two more have just arrived. Is it a problem?"

"I'll manage."

He curled an arm around her shoulders, dropped a kiss on her forehead, then gave her a dazzling smile. "I'll take you out to dinner tomorrow night to compensate."

He left her feeling poleaxed. "Damned womaniser," she muttered to herself. It was a thought that was repeated continually throughout the evening. Women hung on him, if not physically, on his every word. Despite the number of guests, he was the central focus of the party, and that never wavered.

When Dani moved out to the barbecue to start cooking the shelled king prawns in the garlic butter, somehow Cameron was at her side, and the party seemed to naturally gravitate out to the patio area and around what she was doing. He was like the Pied Piper, Dani thought, except these were women following Cameron McFarlane, not plague rats following a musician.

But it worked well because the guests were there to help themselves as soon as she had concocted the first culinary delight from the barbecue. The moment the prawns were ready, Dani poured some warmed olive oil through the pre-cooked *cannellini* to keep them separated, spooned through the caviar, then added the sizzling prawns.

The combination of white beans, black caviar, and red prawns, not only looked great but tasted great as well. Dani transferred the steaming dish to the buffet table where a range of salads stood ready, and Cameron's guests were not backward in coming forward to pounce on the new offering by the chef. Dani allowed herself a smug little smile as she returned to the barbecue to start on the Hawaiian lamb kabobs.

"Delicious. Best prawns I've ever eaten."

She glanced up from her cooking to find herself face to face with a gorgeous blonde with a gaping cleavage. It made Dani glad she hadn't worn her little black dress because it would have made a very poor comparison to the stunningly sexy black dress this woman wore. Dani suspected she was the owner of the black silk lace panties she had found in Cameron's bedroom the day before. It was the same blonde who had been draping herself on Cameron whenever he stood still long enough for her to do so.

Dani forced a smile. "I'm glad you enjoyed them."

"Where did Cameron find you?"

"In his bedroom," Dani answered matter-of-factly. No way was she going to admit to this woman that she'd been cleaning Cameron's house yesterday. And doing her intimate laundry.

The blonde seemed stunned. Dani pointedly returned her attention to the kabobs, which she began to turn over. Let Cameron explain, she thought savagely. If he wanted to. The blonde was his business, not hers.

"When did you meet?"

"Yesterday morning. About nine o'clock."

"That figures."

The edge of bitter irony caused Dani to glance up from her cooking again. The blonde gave her a woman-to-woman little smile.

"He didn't want me to stay the whole night with him." She looked Dani up and down. "So what have you got that I don't have?"

Dani decided to backtrack fast. She didn't want to give the wrong impression and get into an altercation over Cameron McFarlane and his love-life. "I didn't jump into bed with him, if that's what you're thinking," she said bluntly. "Certain circumstances arose and he needed a chef. Which is what I am. Apart from that, I haven't got anything, really. I just go my own way..."

The woman stared at her in disbelief. "You must have something. He's been keeping an eye on you all evening, so I know he's attracted to you."

Dani didn't believe that for a moment, but even if she wanted to believe it, the image of him and Nicole... Dani shuddered. "Too bad!" she said, doing her best to sound casually indifferent. But inside she was feeling confused and disturbed. She kept on turning the kabobs as though that was the only thing that interested her. She wished the blonde would go away.

She didn't. "You are unbelievable," she accused. "Every woman here wants an invitation into his bed."

It exasperated Dani. "Look," she said confidingly, "if you want him, it's all right with me. I don't mind. Really I don't."

"Hell!" said the blonde. She looked dazed and confused beyond belief.

"Anybody here can have him, for all I care." Dani was getting into her stride. "Consider him up for grabs. It means absolutely nothing to me."

"*You* don't mind?" Her jaw was agape.

This was dragging on, and Dani needed to concentrate on her cooking. "What do I have to say? You've got my permission, if that's what you want. Anyone here who wants to bed Cameron McFarlane has got my permission. Now if you don't mind..."

The blonde walked away as though her world had suddenly collapsed.

Dani could only half concentrate on the kabobs, but she had become so automatically good at what she did that even half her mind could produce better results than most people attained with their full minds.

Damn people with silky blond hair and big cleavages, she thought. But she had learned years ago not to compete. She had to use the equipment she was born with to full advantage and let the others with more favoured genetics look after themselves.

The thought that Cameron McFarlane could find her attractive—more attractive than the well-endowed blonde—was too much to credit. If he was keeping an eye on her, it was probably because he was piqued at her resistance to his charm. Which was because of Nicole. Otherwise she would have been mincemeat for him, as Nicole had charmingly suggested.

Perhaps she was an amusing curiosity to him, a subject for a chapter in his next book, another of her sister's sweetly acid suggestions. Or maybe he was merely checking that she was handling his party with the expertise she had promised. He couldn't be truly attracted. The blonde simply wasn't getting the attention *she* wanted from him, and looking for reasons to explain her own failure.

Dani switched off the grill, arranged the kabobs on their serving plates, carried them to the buffet table, then left the guests to their appetites. While they were occupied on the patio she did a fast clean-up in the living room; glasses into the bar dishwasher, trays to the kitchen. All that was left of her hors d'oeuvres were a few curls of celery and carrot sticks which she had placed around and between the rolls of smoked salmon. There wasn't even a scraping left of the avocado dip.

Dani had set out a fine array of cheeses and crackers on trays and was working on the fruit platters when Cameron breezed into the kitchen, beaming benevolence and his strong male charisma. "Need a hand with anything, Dani?"

"No, thank you," she snapped.

It halted him in his stride. "Something wrong?"

"What could be wrong? Your guests are golloping up everything I put in front of them. There are now forty of them instead of twenty. So far I've coped. Under severe difficulties. Any more questions?"

"The food has been superb, Dani. Wonderful. Compliments all around." He was still looking at her quizzically. "Are you angry about the extra guests?"

"I'm not angry about anything. I'm simply doing my job." She shot him a meaning look. "Yours is to entertain your guests. So go on back to it."

He frowned. "Did Simone say something to you?"

"Who's Simone?"

"When you were cooking the kabobs."

"She said the prawns were great. I gave her permission to bed you any time she liked." She nodded towards the cheese and crackers. "You can carry one of those trays to the guests if you want to do something useful."

"You gave her permission?"

He looked dumbfounded.

It gave Dani a sweet sense of satisfaction. "Simone—if that's her name—seemed a bit disturbed. She had the weird idea that you fancied me." Dani rolled her eyes and turned to the fruit platter. "When you give her back her silk lace panties from Thursday night, you might reassure her that I'm not on your list of conquests."

Cameron picked up a tray, then paused. Dani could feel his eyes boring into her, but she didn't look up from the Kiwi fruit she was peeling.

"I think this is getting out of hand," he said, his tone clearly one of vexation.

She shook her head. "It doesn't bother me, Cameron."

"I think I've got some explaining to do..."

"The guests," Dani said pointedly. "And they don't bother me, either. The more people who like what I do, the more satisfaction I get from it."

It was true. Usually. Somehow pleasure in her work was escaping her tonight. She wished Cameron would go and leave her alone. Instead he stepped towards her, put a hand on her shoulder and gave it a gentle squeeze, commanding her attention.

"I like what you do, Dani," he said softly, his blue eyes serious for once, and dark with some deep purpose. "Very much," he added in a low throb. Then he favoured her with his heart-stopping smile and left her to her work.

In a most uncharacteristic burst of frustration, Dani stabbed her peeling knife into a piece of pineapple. Surprised at her own strength of feeling, she lifted the piece of fruit to her mouth and chewed it. Cameron McFarlane was not for her, and that was that. He could switch on all his charm until the cows came home. He was unalterably off her list.

She finished her arrangement of tropical fruits inside the pineapple shells, piled fresh berries around them, interspersed these with chocolate-coated orange peel, then admired her handiwork—artistic and mouth-watering. It was a pity she was feeling so sour with life in general. Without a doubt, her catering was first class.

Dani spent the next hour discreetly cleaning up after the hot courses, filling the dishwasher, emptying it, washing the large trays and serving plates. Music was blaring, people were dancing, and the cheese and fruit were being picked at with relish. From the way things were going, she couldn't anticipate an early end to the party. It was very much in full swing.

At midnight she rolled out the traymobile with the coffee things and her death-by-chocolate cake. Most of the guests partook of both, but as a hint for them to go home, it was a dismal failure. They were still partying on an hour later, and the chocolate cake was all gone.

Dani did another clean-up, then sat in the kitchen drinking coffee. Her job was done. She felt tired and drained and exhausted, totally spent physically, mentally and emotionally. By rights she could go home now. Somehow she didn't want to.

It was nonsense to think she had to speak to Cameron before she went. She didn't have to. But she did want to know if he would accept her decision to release him from his part of the bargain. Would he accept it with relief? Would he argue? Apart from which, there was a dreadful fascination in finding out if Simone was going to lose another pair of knickers tonight. Or would it be someone else?

She was brooding over these highly questionable questions when Cameron swept into the kitchen again. "Business done," he declared. "Time for pleasure. Come and join the party, Dani."

She viewed him with jaundiced eyes. "No, thank you. I'll just wait here and clean up after they're all gone." For some stupid reason she cringed inwardly as she added, "Unless I'd be in the way of, uh, other arrangements."

He grimaced. "Somewhere along the way," he said slowly and seriously, "you have got the wrong idea."

He took her hand, the one that was not curled around the coffee mug. His eyes seemed to say that the only other arrangement he had in mind was with her. Which sent Dani's pulse into a skittish canter. His fingers stroked over hers, pressing their persuasion.

"I wouldn't allow anything to stand in the way of our agreement, Dani. I want you to come and enjoy yourself with me. When everyone's gone, I'll help you clean up, if you insist we have to do it."

Stop it now, Dani's mind screamed. *Right now!* It was the perfect opportunity. Then she could go home with a clear conscience.

Instead she allowed him to draw her off the kitchen stool. Once on her feet she dredged up the energy and willpower to do what had to be done. She began by deliberately extracting her hand from his. He frowned at her pointed disengagement from him.

"There's something I have to tell you, Cameron." She forced the words out determinedly.

"What?"

"The agreement is off. I've decided I don't want you with me on Christmas Day," she rushed on. "You were in a fix over this party, and I wouldn't let you down after giving my word, so I did the job you wanted. But I don't want anything in return from you."

"Why not?" he demanded.

"You're not what I want," she stated flatly. "I've crossed you off my list."

He looked incredulous. "You think I can't do what you want?" The challenge in his voice carried a confidence that aroused Dani's resentment of what she perceived as his careless acquisition of any woman he fancied.

"You think you're God's gift to women," she accused hotly. "Well, let me tell you that my grandmother and my mother and my father will spot you for a fraud in no time flat!"

"The hell they will!" he retorted with strength. "One thing I'm not, and never have been, is a fraud. I wouldn't have got to where I am if I were a fraud. I wouldn't have agreed to our bargain in the first place if I hadn't wanted to be with you."

"And why, might I ask, do you want that?" Dani scoffed.

His anger melted into something more disturbing. "Because you're the most provocative package I've ever been presented with."

Dani was outraged. "I am *not* provocative. I've *never* been provocative. I don't believe in being provocative."

"No?" He raised an eyebrow, but the sternness of his mouth...was it a trace of anger? "Then why have I thought of nothing but you since you woke me up yesterday morning?"

Dani didn't have an answer to that. "I'm *not* a package."

"Yes you are, Dani. A package full of surprises. A package I want to open. And find out all there is to know of what is inside." He moved forward and slid one hand around her waist. "The wrapping is interesting. I want to know what it's hiding."

He was pulling her closer. Dani lifted her hands to his chest to push away. "This isn't a good idea, Cameron," she warned in quick, urgent words.

"It feels good." His other hand completed the encirclement of her waist. His eyes burned into hers, denying there was any ground for her to protest. "I've been wanting to taste that saucy mouth. It begs for exploration."

"No, it's not begging," she choked out. Her throat had gone all tight. It felt paralysed. Her whole body felt paralysed. There was suddenly something very mesmerising about the way his mouth was coming towards hers. She was like a mouse waiting for the predator to strike. She made an enormous effort to concentrate on what had to be done. "I don't think..."

"This is not the time for thinking."

Then his lips were brushing over hers, a soft tingling contact that was both sensual and seductive. Dani struggled with herself. Of course, she couldn't take him home with her on Christmas Day. That was definitely out. And she certainly couldn't have him as a lover. That was just as definitely out. But a kiss... well, there was no harm in that, was there? And she was entitled to it, wasn't she? Just to see what it was like with him?

CHAPTER FIVE

THE QUESTION became academic as Dani lost her train of thought. His mouth was warm and soft and mobile. It didn't feel too badly at all. In fact, it felt very good. And she was far too tired to fight Cameron off.

She had no remorse at leaning more of her weight against him. He appeared to take the slump of fatigue as encouragement, his mouth weaving a symphony of sensation over her lips. He gave her such comforting support that she let herself sag into his secure embrace, pressing her breasts against his chest as his mouth began to work more vigorously over hers. She liked the texture of his lips. Quite instinctively she moved her tongue slowly but fleetingly over their graduating softness.

Cameron McFarlane apparently took this as further encouragement. He started exploring her mouth with his tongue, long sensual rolling movements that were intensely exciting and left her feeling like quivering jelly. She was boneless, weightless, soaring like an eagle, but there were things she wanted to try, things she'd never thought of before, things she had never imagined doing . . . like finding out if it was just as exciting to explore his mouth in the same way.

And her hands itched to do things, too. They played over his neck. She sensed it had something to do with nerves. She didn't know how she knew, but it felt right, and Cameron McFarlane seemed to be responding just right. For some reason he was uttering short little moans, but he was aroused by her touch, no doubt about that. And she felt feline and graceful.

Yes, for the first time in her life she felt graceful, as if her body had been made to belong right where it was, and Cameron led her into an intensely exciting rhythm that united their mouths and stomachs and hips. She liked where she was, she liked what she was doing, she liked what *he* was doing to her. It felt as if her world had gone into overdrive and she was spinning into a new dimension.

She had tried kissing before, but it had not been the same, never like this. The boys had been so gauche, so awkward or so greedy to take. Whether it was their lack of giving, or the fact that she had not been so involved emotionally to be all-giving, the result was the same. Dani never had any trouble repulsing physical advances that didn't please her.

Nicole was half right. She was a virgin. But she was definitely *not* foolish about it. It had never felt right before, and why should she give sufferance to something that didn't feel right? It was not that she lacked curiosity or confidence in herself. She simply refused to give a man pleasure that he could not return. That was one of the lessons she had learnt from the women's movement over the past twenty years—a woman had rights. And Dani believed in exercising them.

One of Cameron's hands trailed up and down the curve of her spine, caressing a shivery line of pleasure. Then it found another line, moving under her upstretched arm and stroking the soft swelling edge of her breast. Dani had an irresistible urge to touch him, too. Ever since she had first seen him she had secretly wondered how it might be.

Experimentally she ran her hands down Cameron McFarlane's back. She felt his muscles contract... ripple. This man was sensitive. Temptation urged her on. She eased her body back a little so that she could bring a hand up to the open neckline of his sports shirt. The buttons seemed to fall open for her. She felt his skin goose prickle under her touch. Her mental and emotional fatigue washed away in a drugging sense of her own pleasure. It was marvellous that he responded like this. He really responded to what a man should respond to.

A numb amazement spread through her mind. No wonder women chased him in droves. He seemed to be instinctively tuned to their needs. A man in a million. But how could she possibly keep him when he had such attributes? He probably *was* God's gift to women. And she couldn't have him, anyhow.

Regret ran through her like a river of lead. She had to stop this. Yet she couldn't cut this kiss off abruptly. Not the kiss of a lifetime. As sad as it was, though, she had to end it.

Intuitively he knew what she was doing and he didn't resist. The pressure of his mouth lightened until their lips were barely grazing. They moved apart, came back to taste the sweet temptation of each other time and time again, intoxicating little frissons of magical electricity, sipping at the entrancing pleasure.

Then Dani lowered her head for the last time and leant it against the warm haven between his shoulder and chest.

His voice was husky as his lips feathered past her ear. "Let's go to bed," he whispered.

There was no question about what she wanted to do. Her stomach, her breasts, her nerves were screaming out for more of the same kind of enthralling experience. It was only with considerable difficulty that Dani forced into her unwilling mind the image of Nicole with him. But she did it. This was the time for sanity. She had to put a stop to what was going on between them and what he was suggesting. Decisively. No matter how hard it was. She remembered a line from *My Fair Lady* and it tripped off her tongue.

"Not bloody likely."

That should do the trick, she thought. And to help it have its decisive effect she mustered up what strength she could and took a step backwards, away from his wandering hands and arms.

Cameron McFarlane looked dazed, drugged, bewildered. "What did you say?"

"Not bloody likely," Dani repeated for him.

Still he couldn't seem to comprehend that she was rejecting the idea of going to bed with him. "What?" he asked incredulously.

If ever there was a time for firmness, this was it, even though she was shaking inside. "The answer is no," Dani said emphatically.

He shook his head as though to clear it. "I was getting a different message a few moments ago."

"I was checking you out."

"You were checking me out?" His voice was strangled with disbelief.

"To see how good you were at kissing."

"And?"

"You were surprisingly good."

"So?"

"That's all. I don't want anything more from you. I don't want to see you again."

"Why?"

"There are reasons..."

"What reasons?"

Dani found it very difficult to say. The question conjured up images that turned her stomach.

"Forget it," she said. "Go find Simone."

"I can't forget it. I don't want Simone."

He sounded very passionate about it. Dani thought the only thing to do was give him some down-to-earth practical advice. "Then sleep by yourself, Cameron. Do you good for a change."

"Tell me what's wrong!"

Quite clearly he wasn't in the mood for taking advice. He seemed angry. Very angry. Dani sighed. Nothing she touched ever turned to gold. At the present moment, everything she touched turned into a disaster. There may as well be another one, she thought, feeling more miserable than she had about everything else. But the truth was the truth. She gave it to him, right between the eyes.

"You slept with my sister." And you can't put spilled milk back in the bottle, Dani thought as she fiercely added, "As far as I'm concerned, that ruins anything there could be between you and me."

A primitive pride blazed from her eyes as she watched Cameron McFarlane pass beyond the initial shock of having to face up to the consequences of his actions. She saw the resentment of being made to pay for something he didn't care about, the burning frustration of not getting his own way, and finally the determination to pursue what he wanted despite everything she had said.

He didn't like rejection, she thought. He had been aroused. Maybe he'd never been rejected before by a woman when he was aroused. He certainly didn't like it. It wasn't necessary to be a professional psychoanalyst to feel that. Yet he didn't have to suffer the physical frustration she was feeling. He could walk straight back to his party and find solace with his pick of any number of women. Including Simone.

Although that kiss had been an incredible revelation to Dani, it couldn't have been so amazingly special to him. For a man of his experience, there'd probably be nothing new left to feel. He'd done it all before, countless times. With her sister, as well. No matter what he said or did, Dani was not about to forget that. She had gone as far as she could let herself go with him. This little episode in her life had to be finished with now.

"I'm going to ring for a taxi," she stated firmly.

"No, you're not!" Ruthless determination tightened his jaw. "Not until we've got this situation sorted out."

"There's nothing to sort out," Dani corrected him. "What's done is done."

"I can see that," he agreed with her. "And it was done between the time you left me yesterday and your arrival here today. Which accounts for the change in your attitude towards me, your intense concentration on your work this afternoon and the flack you've been giving me tonight. Right?"

"Right!" she snapped, finding his analysis distasteful in the circumstances.

"Right!" he snapped back at her. "Now who the hell is your sister? To my certain knowledge I have never slept with a woman by the name of Halstead." His eyes blazed over her. "Although I most certainly want to."

Dani instantly felt a deep and bitter resentment on her sister's behalf that he couldn't remember her name. It was totally damning. No doubt about it, he was nothing more than a rooster in a henhouse. Nicole was right. He only used women for his own purposes, and that was the end of it. He didn't care enough to remember them afterwards.

"My sister's name is Nicole. Nicole Halstead. I daresay you didn't get as far as her surname," she answered coldly.

"I know *everything* about every woman with whom I've shared any intimacy," he retorted with grim authority. "I do not know a Nicole Halstead."

"You do so!" Dani told him in towering disgust at his lies.

"I tell you I don't know," he insisted in angry challenge. "If you're so sure of your facts, tell me when and where."

"Nicole works for the PR company that promotes your books in Australia," Dani recited accusingly. "Does that jog your insultingly blank memory?"

It still took him a few moments to make a connection. Then he said with a look of total perplexity, "*That* Nicole?"

He sounded incredulous, which put Dani slightly off her stride. "She happens to be my sister," she reminded him fiercely.

It was a warning. No matter how mean and bitchy Nicole might be, Dani had a very strong sense of family loyalty, and she was not about to allow Cameron McFarlane to put her sister down any more than he had already done by supposedly not remembering her.

There was not one wavering flicker in the blue eyes that glittered at her with triumphant satisfaction. "She was introduced to me as Nicky. I didn't learn her last name. If it was ever given. And I have not slept with your sister," he declared with ringing conviction. "Never. Not once."

Dani's eyes narrowed. "How do you know you haven't? You obviously can't remember."

"My memory is faultless on people I have met. Your sister is a slight—*very* slight—business acquaintance. She has never been, and never will be, anything more than that in my life," he said emphatically. "To put it succinctly, she is not on my list."

"Your *list!*" Dani snorted in contempt.

His eyes derided her contempt. "You have a list. I have a list. And I don't care to be crossed off *your* list because of some mistaken notion that your sister is on *my* list."

This put Dani in a fix. She didn't want to tell him that hers was an imaginary list. Besides, they were getting off the point. "How come Nicole says you did sleep with her?"

"How would I know why Nicole says I did?"

"You're accusing my sister of being a liar."

"I think she's very much mistaken. Or..."

"Or what?"

One eyebrow rose. "Or your sister has a very vivid imagination."

To Dani's certain knowledge, Nicole had no imagination at all. And she didn't make mistakes. Her sister was utterly dedicated to facts and figures, which she threw at Dani at every opportunity. So one or the other of them was lying. The trick was, which one?

She eyed Cameron McFarlane suspiciously. He looked very confident of being in control again. But he was supposed to be a master of psychology. Having been thrown off stride himself, it would be an effective counterstrike to throw her off stride.

"I'll think about it," she said.

"Dani, if I went out on the patio and swore black, blue and brindle that you hopped into bed with me yesterday morning, don't you think most people would believe it?"

"Probably," Dani acknowledged reluctantly.

"That's the position I'm in," he said persuasively. "How can I prove I didn't do something?"

He had a point. But he could still be lying. Yet if it was Nicole who was lying... Why, why, why would she do that?

"I don't like you very much," she said, half to herself. Although it wasn't true. If Nicole had told a great big lie, she could get to like Cameron McFarlane a great deal. Too much, really. Which would lead to another inevitable disaster.

His hands were on her shoulders, softly kneading them. "You did like me yesterday, Dani. After we made our bargain, you were beginning to like me quite a lot." He raised a challenging eyebrow, and the blue eyes bored into hers. "Are you going to let a lie spoil what we could have together?"

Dani's stomach churned with uncertainty. She wished she could give in to the temptation of his touch, to let him be close to her again. The memory of how it had felt with him clouded her thinking. She struggled to regain good, sound reasoning. If Nicole had lied... But then, there was Simone, as well. How could she know what was true or not?

"You like blondes," she stated accusingly.

"I don't like blondes!" Cameron rasped in exasperation. "I don't care what colour a woman's hair is. It can be black, red, green, purple...." He paused to catch his breath.

"They're all the same to you as long as they perform in bed," Dani finished for him.

The pupils of his eyes seemed to contract. "You've got the wrong idea about me, Dani," he bit out.

"In what way?" she asked sceptically.

"I like women. As people. I like you as a person."

"And Simone?"

"Is a very nice person. But I'm not in love with her."

Dani stared at him.

He shrugged. "Simone is doing her doctorate. We have had a mutually satisfying relationship. There is no commitment to each other on either side." He paused, his eyes boring into hers. "Something wrong with that?"

Dani was fairly sure Simone would have liked a commitment, but Dani was not here to fight Simone's battles. She shrugged. "That's your business. It has nothing to do with me."

He sighed. Heavily. Then very softly he said, "I want *you*, Dani." And the desire warming his eyes made mincemeat of Dani's stomach.

Fortunately her brain was still in reasonable working order. Right now he wanted her. Dani couldn't disbelieve that. But only a couple of nights ago he had wanted Simone. And before that, her sister? How many other women had contributed to his list? Dani really didn't care to be part of a list.

"Why should my sister lie to me?" she demanded.

He shook his head. "God knows! You'll have to ask her. Maybe she's jealous of you. I don't know."

This wasn't getting her anywhere. "I'll think about it," she said again.

Desire slid swiftly into speculation. "I don't know for certain what's on your sister's mind. I do know for certain I'm telling the truth," Cameron stated decisively. "I did not sleep with your sister. I was not even tempted to sleep with your sister. Perhaps she resented that. She let me know, in the subtle way that women have, that she was available if needed. I did not react to it because I do not take up with any woman on the basis of her giving me the green light. Believe it or not, I do have a strong sense of discrimination as to what I want, when I want it and with whom."

Dani considered all of this for several moments. Maybe he wasn't quite the womaniser Nicole had painted him. He wasn't exactly celibate, either. However, it was hardly reasonable to expect a man of his years not to have had a few relationships in the past. If Cameron McFarlane was telling the truth, if he really had rejected Nicole's come-on and preferred her, Dani Halstead... A glorious light switched on in Dani's brain, and Cameron McFarlane went up in her estimation like a supersonic elevator.

One question came uppermost to mind. "Why me, then?"

He smiled. It was a winning smile. A smile that radiated happiness and well-being. A smile that Dani decided she'd better be suspicious of, because it was doing a lot of damage to her inside, and that could be very dangerous if he was an out-and-out liar.

"You're enchanting. Natural, uninhibited, and with a deliciously tart dash of spice. After that kiss we shared, I have a strong feeling that we fit together."

"Well, I'm not too sure I find you enchanting, Cameron," she quickly derided. "Or that we fit together all that well." The suspicion remained, however, that he could be right. And if he really, *really* preferred her to Nicole... "I'm going to check back with Nicole and hear her side of this before I'll consider being enchanted by you." She paused and raised her eyebrows. "Can you live with that?"

The smile turned into a grimace. Frustration tightened his face. He finally relaxed into a resigned sigh, his eyes mocking the resolution in hers. "I guess this means you won't be staying the night."

"As I said before, I'm going to ring for a taxi."

"I'll take you home."

"No, you won't. You've got guests to tend to."

"Damn the guests! They can look after themselves."

"That's very selfish. You invited them."

"Only half of them."

"That's not the point. You're the host. Besides, I don't want you taking me home. I don't know yet if I want to be with you or not. And until I make up my mind about that..."

"Dani, I've told you the truth," he appealed with an edge of strong feeling.

"If it's the truth, it will still be the truth tomorrow, and the next day, and the next day," she argued. "Think of it this way, Cameron. You may not want me by then, anyway. And that will settle things for both of us."

"You like having things your own way, Dani Halstead," he grated between his teeth.

"A woman has to do what a woman has to do," Dani tossed off.

His chagrin crumbled into a ripple of soft laughter. "Why fight it?" he said, lifting his hands from her shoulders and shaking his head. "Take your taxi, if you must. Tomorrow is another day." His eyes flared with the promise that they would meet again . . . and with a different outcome.

Whether that was male pride or serious intent, Dani couldn't be absolutely sure. She knew that she very definitely needed a breathing space to work things out in her own way.

He insisted on giving her money for the taxi fare, which Dani readily accepted since she had done a great deal of work for him and it wasn't by any means sure that she would get any compensation for it. That remained a very grey area for the present.

There were still some fifteen or so guests lingering at the party—Simone amongst them—when the taxi arrived. Cameron made a point of escorting Dani to the waiting cab. "Thanks for all the work you put in, Dani," he said as he saw her settled onto the back seat. He made no reference to tomorrow.

She looked at him, a flash of cynicism in her eyes. "It was an interesting experience, Cameron," she said, but her heart was heavy.

Cameron touched his fingers to his lips and threw her a kiss as he shut the door. It was a charming gesture. He was very good at charm. Very good at everything.

She didn't look back as the taxi moved forward. The equation was very clear to Dani. If Cameron Mc-

Farlane truly wanted her, he would come after her. On the other hand, if he had been lying through his teeth in order to win some brief satisfaction tonight, he knew the game was up and there was no point in pursuing her even if he wanted to. Either way, nothing could be settled until tomorrow, so there wasn't much point in thinking about it.

For some reason Dani had a blinding headache by the time she arrived home. She was not prone to headaches. It must be because of having all her emotions scrambled around, Dani decided.

She took a quick shower, pulled on her nightie, then undid the tightly woven plait and fluffed her hair out, hoping that might ease the problem. As an extra measure, she took two aspirin tablets before falling into bed.

She tried to go to sleep, but she couldn't help thinking about that kiss and remembering how it had felt. She wished she could know all that might have followed on from it. She figured that would be very worthwhile knowing. At least once in a lifetime.

She was only twenty-three years old, she consoled herself, and Cameron McFarlane couldn't be the only man in the world who knew how to respond to a woman. If she couldn't have him, that was that. Nevertheless—although it wasn't a nice thing to contemplate—she wouldn't mind too much if she found out Nicole had misled her.

And if it was true Cameron McFarlane wasn't the rooster in the henhouse she thought he was, well, she wouldn't mind that, either.

Of course, neither factor would have any meaning at all if he didn't come after her. Dani was through with counting chickens before they hatched. No doubt about it. As Grandma said, a bird in the hand was always worth two in the bush.

Somehow this piece of wisdom did nothing to ease the dull throbbing pain in her head and heart.

CHAPTER SIX

DANI WAS DREAMING about chasing birds through a confusing wilderness of bushes when a banging on her front door woke her up. It was a relief to get out of that dream. For some reason she had birds on the brain.

She squinted at her bedside clock, which showed it was almost ten. But it was Sunday morning, and she wasn't expecting any visitors. If it was Mrs. B she would have come to the stairwell door not the outside one. So it couldn't be her or one of the upstairs couple. Unless perhaps one of them had accidentally locked himself or herself out of the house. That had happened before, particularly after a raging argument.

Dani dragged herself out of bed. At least her headache had dissipated overnight. The morning could be faced without wincing. She drew on her cotton robe, pushed her hair away from her face, then went to the door to answer the summons, which persisted.

Dani could hardly believe her eyes when she found Cameron McFarlane on the basement landing. His handsome face instantly beamed with pleasure at seeing her. Because of her untidy state Dani was half-hidden behind the door, but that was no protection.

His smile was bright enough to dizzy her, and the rest of him—in blue jeans and a white cotton pullover—emanated vibrant vitality.

"What are you doing here?" she asked dazedly.

"It's tomorrow," he replied. "The sun is shining. It's a beautiful day. I've come to take you out with me."

She stared at him, struggling with the temptation he held out. He *had* come after her. Which meant he really did want her, didn't it?

But she still didn't know if he'd been lying about Nicole or not.

"You woke me up," she said, stating the obvious while she tried to get her thoughts in order. "I'm not dressed," she added, self-consciously aware that her body was singing its own treacherous song of excited pleasure at having Cameron here with her in the light of another day.

His eyebrows slanted appealingly. "I did allow you eight hours' sleep. Which is more than I got, tossing and turning and thinking of you. Throw some clothes on, Dani, and let's take off."

Dani paused for serious consideration. Her hand automatically went to her hair.

"Don't worry about your hair," he urged. "It's beautiful the way it is."

Beautiful? It must be a mess, Dani thought. And Cameron was bombarding her with charm. She frowned at him. "I haven't rung Nicole yet."

"Then do it right now." Something feral glittered into the blue eyes. "In fact, I'd like to speak to her myself."

No, Dani thought. This is between Nicole and me. Private family business. And a serious matter, as well. At least to Dani, it was. If Nicole had vilified Cameron McFarlane's character out of malice and spite, that was very disturbing. After all, they were sisters.

"I want to speak to Nicole alone, Cameron," she said decisively.

He hesitated, obviously reluctant to let that happen. His eyes burned into hers, reminding her of how they had felt together, reminding her of all he was offering her. Dani felt extremely conscious of not being properly dressed. Her body, under the free-flowing nightie and robe, was remembering all the sensations of last night's embrace, and the desire to explore that experience further was little short of overwhelming. Perhaps Cameron sensed it and was satisfied with his effect on her. He relaxed into another charming smile.

"Go to it, then. I'll drop in on Mrs. B and have a little chat with her. I expect you to be ready to go when I come back."

Dani hastily closed the door and leaned against it, taking several deep breaths to calm her racing pulse and pump some strength into her legs. Cameron McFarlane certainly was dynamite when he chose to exert the power of his attraction. She shouldn't have let him kiss her, Dani thought. It had closed the distance between them with devastating force. Distance that she had to keep if Nicole had not been lying.

Dani pushed herself away from the door and headed for the telephone. She dialled her sister's number, feverishly hoping Nicole had not gone out this morning, because she didn't know what she would do if the burning question couldn't be resolved. That Cameron had wanted to speak to Nicole suggested he was innocent. Or did it? Perhaps he had the power and influence to threaten Nicole's career. Dani suspected that Cameron McFarlane could be very ruthless when it came to getting his own way.

Did he really find her so attractive?

Or was it a case of not being finished with her until *he* decided he was finished?

Answer me, Nicole, Dani thought with growing impatience as she waited for the telephone receiver to be picked up at the other end of the line. It felt like an interminable length of time before it was. Yet when Nicole's voice did answer the call, Dani was immediately plunged into a ferment of uncertainty. How was she to ask if her sister had lied about Cameron? It was so shaming and offensive, whatever the outcome.

"Who's calling, please?" Aggrieved.

"It's Dani," she blurted. "I...I need to know if you said those things about Cameron because...because you wanted to protect me from being hurt."

Silence.

"Nicole? Please? I really need to know," Dani appealed desperately.

More silence. Then, tersely, "If you're intent on making a fool of youself over Cameron McFarlane, Dani, go right ahead. The decision is yours."

Dani sighed. The metaphorical washing of hands. Which wouldn't do in this case. "Look, Nicole," she tried again. "Maybe I'm not the kind of sister you'd like to have. We don't seem to have much in common. But this is important to me. You see—" there was no way around it, she had to say it straight out "—you see...Cameron swears he didn't sleep with you."

"You asked him?" Shock, swiftly escalating to outrage. "How dare you talk to him about me! How dare you..." Nicole choked on her fury.

Dani winced. Why hadn't she thought of the bitter wound to Nicole's pride? If Cameron McFarlane was telling the truth... "I'm sorry," she rushed out. "I didn't ask him, Nicole. He kind of pressured me into giving him the reason I was refusing to...to see him any more. And he swore that he hadn't had that kind of interest with you."

"And you believe him." Blistering resentment.

"Nicole..." Desperate appeal. "I didn't know what to believe. I thought maybe..."

"Believe what you like, Dani."

It was now Nicole's turn to crash the telephone receiver down and put an emphatic end to pursuing the painful point any further.

Dani felt both frustrated and deeply disturbed as she slowly returned the receiver to its cradle. Nothing would ever be the same again. She had given Nicole the ultimate insult. If Cameron McFarlane had rejected Nicole, and really wanted her, Dani, then Nicole would certainly consider that the greatest insult she had received in her life.

Why did it have to be like this? Why couldn't she and Nicole be friends? Nicole treated her almost as if she was a competitor, yet Dani had gone out of her way *not* to compete with Nicole. Tears burned her eyes

as she removed her hand from the telephone. She felt
chewed up inside. A mess.

She probably shouldn't have doubted her sister's
word. She should never have revealed what Nicole had
said to Cameron McFarlane, shaming her sister just
because he got under her skin. Dani didn't have to see
him again, but Nicole undoubtedly would in the
course of her work at the PR company. Why hadn't
she thought of that?

Nicole would never forgive her. Never in a million
years. Nicole may not have liked Dani much before,
but now she would hate her. The burning tears welled
up and overflowed. Dani slumped on her bed in de-
feat. Another disaster. Nothing turned out right for
her. Not ever.

But there was no point in sitting here moaning and
groaning about the situation. She had to make up her
mind what to do about Cameron. He would be coming back for her soon. Dani got herself moving while
she thought about Cameron McFarlane's persistence.

She had a quick wash then hurried through her
dressing, automatically choosing her favourite skirt
and matching blouse. It was not an expensive outfit,
only polished cotton, but the tiny floral print in oranges and greens and browns suited her colouring, and
Dani was not completely without vanity. Whatever she
decided to do about Cameron McFarlane, some core
of feminine pride inside her wanted him to see her
looking nice for once. She quickly fastened the stylish
belt in tan leather around her small waist and slid the
matching sandals onto her feet.

When the expected knock came on her door, Dani was sliding a couple of combs above her ears, bringing some order to the mass of waves and curls that tumbled to her shoulder-blades. Her bathroom mirror reflected a pale face, and the freckles across her nose and cheekbones seemed to stand out more than usual. Could a man like Cameron McFarlane really want *her?* Dani asked herself. Had Nicole lied out of spite and jealousy?

Damn Nicole! Dani thought fiercely. She'd been interfering in *her* life, *all* her life, making her feel second-rate and not worthy of notice. For whatever reason he had, Cameron McFarlane was certainly taking notice of her. And if Dani wiped everything else out, the plain unvarnished truth was she *wanted* to be with Cameron McFarlane. She *wanted* to explore the amazing and exciting sense of rightness with him.

Having made her decision, Dani applied a soft coral lipstick to put some colour on her face, then went to confront the man whose desire for her was about to be measured.

She opened the door and was once more swamped by the impact of his compelling physical presence. His blue eyes glittered with pleasure as they took in her appearance, and the smile he gave her was a force-ten heart stopper.

"Great! You're ready."

Dani took a quick breath to ease the constriction in her chest. "More or less," she said evasively.

"Nicole came clean."

He said that with such confidence it was difficult not to assume he was innocent. But being a master psychologist, he might have worked out that Nicole had a career to protect. It was not conclusive.

"More or less," Dani replied, even more evasively.

"So now you know you can trust me."

"That might be overstating the case a trifle."

"Learn to trust your instincts, Dani." The advice had a liberal coating of self-satisfaction.

Trusting her instincts was one thing that Dani was *not* going to do. That could be far too dangerous with this man. She took a deep breath and asked, "What have you got in mind for today, Cameron? You didn't say earlier."

"How about a swim? It's hot now, and it can only get hotter. Unless there's something specific you'd like to do, we can laze around the pool today, then go out for dinner this evening." He grinned. "Consider me your slave for the day. Tell me what you want and I'll give it to you."

"That sounds fair," Dani said, unable to stop herself from responding to his flirtatious grin. "I'll collect the things I need."

A few moments later Dani joined him on the basement landing with her beach bag. Her heart was pumping so excitedly that she was already locking the door behind her before she remembered Mrs. B and her bad ankle. She shot Cameron a look of appeal.

"Would you mind waiting a bit longer? I should check on Mrs. B to see if she needs anything."

"No need. She's mobile again. One could almost say spritely." His eyes danced with amusement. "Besides which, she has company. A gentleman by the name of Henry Newbold. He's taking Mrs. B out to lunch.''

"Oh! How lovely for her!''

Dani was so pleased for her friend that she barely noticed Cameron relieving her of her beach bag, but she certainly noticed his arm sliding around her waist as they went up the basement steps together. Her whole body was vibrantly alive to the warmth of his hand on her hip, and the brush of his body against hers was oddly mesmerising. Dani did not recollect her wits until she was seated in the front passenger seat of Cameron's car.

Why did it feel so different with him, Dani wondered, perplexed and disturbed by the intensity of the response his touch drew from her. She could be in big trouble before this day was out if she didn't put some firm control on proceedings. If Cameron thought last night's kiss represented a go-ahead signal, she had to scotch that idea immediately. Otherwise lazing around his pool might lead to all kinds of complications, including his bed.

It was all very well feeling strongly attracted to him, but she didn't want to end up being used for a chapter in his new book. For the life of her, she couldn't understand why he should choose to want *her* above Nicole. Or Simone, for that matter. It made no sense to her.

Cameron took his seat beside her. The closing of his door seemed to lend an intimate atmosphere to their togetherness. Dani frowned at him as he flashed her a smile that expressed far too much satisfaction for her comfort.

"I'm still not sure I like you," she blurted out, feeling a need to prick his confidence.

"Today's the perfect opportunity for you to find out that you do," he replied, not the least bit pricked.

"I'm coming because you owe me a day," Dani declared, spelling out the terms for his conduct.

That seemed to galvanize his attention. The blue eyes speared into hers. "Am I to understand Christmas Day is still off, Dani?"

She grimaced. "Well, it won't work any more, Cameron. It would cause trouble within the family, and I don't want to do that."

"I see," he said grimly. "So Nicole didn't back off."

"In a way she did," Dani assured him quickly. "But she knows you, Cameron, and that spoils the effect I wanted. Whether it's true or not, you have a reputation of being a womaniser, so it won't do me any good to turn up with you."

He frowned. "What effect did you want?"

"To turn the spotlight of interest onto you instead of me. You happen to be the archetype of all the qualities my family admires." She shrugged. "Hopelessly superficial, of course, but that's the way they judge."

"Superficial..." The word clearly stuck in his throat.

"You know...handsome face, good physique, highly successful in your chosen career, rolling in money, smart dresser, charming manner..."

"Those qualities mean nothing to you?" he asked, a quirky little smile on his lips.

"Oh, I wouldn't knock them. I was quite prepared to use them," Dani acknowledged. "But compared to other things, I don't think they're terribly important."

"Like what?"

"Having a good heart, kindness, honesty, loyalty, fidelity... things like that."

He flashed her a challenging look. "It will be interesting to see how honest *you* are, Dani."

Which gave her food for thought as he started the car and drove them toward a day of highly questionable togetherness. She wanted him. There was no denying that. But people could want a lot of things that were not good for them.

"What was the difference of opinion that caused you to leave your job at Julio's?" Cameron inquired, surprising her out of her worrisome reverie.

It was a safe subject, Dani decided. She explained what had happened with Julio and how disillusioned she felt with the whole business.

Cameron made sympathetic comments that sounded sincere. Then he slanted her an inquiring look. "So what are you going to do now?"

Dani shrugged. "I haven't made up my mind yet."

He smiled as though he was pleased she had no immediate plan. "I'm sure something will turn up," he said.

Not for her, Dani thought. *He* might be lucky, but she wasn't. She needed to prove herself on every job she obtained, and none of them had come easy.

When they came to a halt at Cameron's house, Dani felt ridiculously nervous about getting out of the car.

It had been a bad idea to come here, she thought. She should have insisted on a public beach. Or somewhere public.

Cameron, however, made no attempt to touch her when she alighted. He led the way into the house, keeping to a relaxed charming manner as he invited her to use the guest suite she had used last night for changing her clothes.

There were a few moments of high tension when she went out to the patio in her bathing suit and saw him in his. Dani had more than enough curves in the right places and her yellow maillot displayed all of them. Cameron showed a fascinated interest in mentally mapping every one. At the same time, Dani couldn't help staring at him in the light of what she had felt in last night's embrace.

It was Cameron who broke the dangerous enthralment, moving not toward her but away, inviting her to share the pool with him. The cold water was a good dampener for more than the summer day's heat. They swam and floated and swam some more. Cameron gradually put her at ease with a mixture of good humour and charm, laughing at things she said and never letting their conversation flag long enough for any discomfiting silences to develop. He seemed interested in her ideas and experiences, and he readily reciprocated with stories of his own.

He did not act or talk like a womaniser, Dani thought with relief. She slowly came to the realisation that the only evidence she had of his womanising was his relationship with Simone, which had been a mutual affair.

She remembered his insistence that he did not bed women indiscriminately. On the other hand, how had he gathered the material for his book *The Psychology of Sex?* That seemed to suggest a lot of first-hand experience. Dani decided she had better get hold of his book and read it for herself.

He undermined other preconceptions she had by cheerfully making them salad sandwiches for lunch and proving himself perfectly capable in the kitchen. He drank a soft drink with her, not criticising her choice or attempting to persuade her into trying anything alcoholic. Dani could not have asked for a more considerate host, nor a more pleasant and stimulating companion. She could not help liking him. Very much.

They were relaxing on the sun loungers after lunch and Dani was feeling a lovely warm contentment when Cameron indirectly reopened the question about Nicole. "Family is important to you, isn't it, Dani," he remarked, rather than asked. His eyes shot her a look of warm approval that Dani found a bit confusing, since one of her family had supposedly maligned him.

"Yes, it is," she replied staunchly, then tried to get the subject on an impersonal level. "I think everyone has a need to feel part of something. Roots of one kind or another. I guess you must miss that, not having a family yourself."

A sardonic smile curled his mouth and his eyes went hard. "Some things are better missed."

"What happened, Cameron?" she asked impulsively. "How did you come to be so alone?"

He shrugged dismissively. "Ancient history, Dani. Tell me about your family." He flashed her a curious look. "Do you love them?"

"Yes." She gave him an ironic smile. "Although sometimes I don't like them too well. Except for Grandma. Grandma is special. When I grow old I want to be just like my grandmother."

Warmth crept into his eyes and seemed to caress her. "Why?"

Dani took a deep breath and tried to ignore the tingly feeling running riot through her body. "Because she's so wise and loving and doesn't try to interfere. She believes in letting people live their own lives, but if you ask her for guidance, she helps without being bossy. I've had some of the best times of my life with Grandma."

"Where does she live?"

"On a little five-acre farm outside Camden. It used to be a much bigger farm, but most of it was sold off to land developers after Grandpa died. Grandma held on to enough so she can still keep her dogs and goats and chickens and have her fruit trees and vegetable garden. Mum and Dad are always on at her to sell up and settle in a retirement village close to them—" she flashed him a triumphant grin "—but no-one's going to get Grandma to do anything she doesn't want to do."

Cameron grinned. "A very strong character?"

"Very independent. Dad says she's old, stubborn and just plain ornery, but there's nothing feeble-minded about Grandma."

In fact, her pithy comments on life often discomfited her family, particularly Nicole, who thought she knew better than anyone. But Dani didn't want to mention Nicole to Cameron.

"Is she your father's mother?"

"No. My mother's. Dad's parents are dead. We never saw much of them. Usually we went to Grandma's for school holidays."

"What did you do there?"

Dani regaled him with stories from her childhood. Cameron listened with such fascinated interest that Dani had the strong impression his childhood had been very different to hers. She wanted to ask him about it, but he skilfully blocked every attempt she made, turning the conversation back to her life. Not that she minded telling him, but she was conscious of him learning a great deal about her and telling very little about himself.

All the same, it was a most enjoyable afternoon. It was only as she was changing to go out to dinner with him that she realised Cameron could have been playing some masterly game of psychology, beaming interest and approval at her to persuade her into revealing so much. On the other hand, why would he want to know if he wasn't really interested?

Cameron took her to a little French restaurant in Paddington and he told her stories of the strange meals he'd had in foreign places. He had her laughing and enjoying herself so much she didn't stop to think his experience was so much wider than hers that she couldn't possibly be a match for him. His eyes kept telling her he was enjoying her response to him, and Dani felt giddy with pleasure.

The meal they had was fine and beautifully presented, and as it turned out, Dani was well acquainted with the chef, having worked with him before she moved on and up to Julio's. She sent him her compliments via their waiter.

In his typically flamboyant style, Henri appeared in the dining room a few minutes later, calling out her name as though she were a long-lost relative. Dani laughingly rose from her chair to be greeted by smacking kisses on both cheeks. Then, of course, she had to introduce Cameron, who looked on with tolerant amusement while Henri poured forth a torrent of words.

"I have heard everything! Julio, upsetting you like that. Deplorable, *cherie*. Terrible. He should be guillotined for disturbing an artist such as yourself. You were right to leave. It is Julio's loss. Who else can make so well the apple pie with the crushed almond pastry? Who else . . ."

"Your pear and ginger pudding is not to be scoffed at, Henri," Dani replied, cheered by his championship.

He made a smacking sound with his lips, tried to look modest and failed hopelessly. "Ah, my Dani! What times we had together! A kitchen with both of us. Let it be so again. If you have not yet secured another position, join me here. I realise it would be a step down for you, *ma cherie,* but our reputation is growing. Who knows where the future may take us? Together we would be strong . . ." Henri looked towards the ceiling with the air of a man who was vouchsafed a vision that would change the world.

The offer took Dani by surprise. She hesitated, but above all else she needed a job. "That's so kind of you, Henri. But impulsive. Don't you think..."

"No!" said Cameron.

"The marvellous things we would create!" enthused Henri, kissing her again.

Dani was doubly distracted.

"Don't do it," said Cameron. "Don't even think about it."

"Why not?" asked Dani.

"Is there some reason?" Henri inquired, forced to take notice of Cameron.

"I've found a job for Dani."

The flat declaration startled both of them.

"You have?" Dani queried disbelievingly.

"The perfect job for you," Cameron asserted.

Dani turned to Henri in some confusion of mind. "Henri, I have to think about this."

"Of course! Think all you like. But you and I, *cherie*. That is worth thinking of. The masterpieces we would create..." He wandered off with the air of a man besotted by his own creations.

Dani sank back onto her chair and looked searchingly at Cameron. He appeared very serious. Had someone in the trade been at the party last night? Or someone who knew someone? Was that why he had been sure something would turn up for her? But why hadn't he told her about it earlier?

"What job have you found for me?"

"One where you can do as you please."

"That sounds good."

"You will have complete control."

Dani's eyebrows shot up. That was unusual. Dani had found a great deal of ego and megalomania in all the kitchens she had worked. Even Henri was temperamental. "You mean I'll be in absolute charge of everything?" she asked incredulously.

"Absolute authority. Total freedom of choice."

"That sounds great." Dani leaned forward eagerly, her eyes sparkling with excitement. "When do I start?"

"Tomorrow."

"Where?"

"At my place. As my personal chef."

Dani's excitement fizzled out. She came back to earth with a thump, all her suspicions about him charging through her mind. Cameron had led her right down the garden path, flattering her, entrancing her, breaking down barriers with consummate skill, but she wasn't so naive that she couldn't see *come in, sucker* written all over this offer. He had wanted her to go to bed with him last night, and this was clearly the next step to achieving that end.

"You can't afford me," she said disdainfully.

His eyes glittered a derisive challenge. "Yes, I can."

"Maybe you can, but I don't want it."

"Why not?"

"It's a live-in position."

"Yes."

"And something else is going to be involved besides cooking."

"Does that frighten you?"

"Any sensible person would be wary of a job like that, where tenure doesn't depend on the quality of the cooking," she mocked. "Besides which, you're flying off to the U.S. on Boxing Day, so it's hardly worth my while to tie myself up with you, is it?"

"Perhaps I won't go. Perhaps I'll want to take my personal chef with me. Consider it a trial run, Dani. A checking-out process, if you like. You'll be well paid for the work, so you won't be out of pocket."

Dani favoured him with a look of arch scepticism. "You may have had a lot of trial runs in your life, Cameron, but let me tell you, they're not my style."

"I said you had complete freedom of choice, Dani. I give you my word that nothing will happen that you don't want to happen."

"How good is your word?" she scoffed.

"As good as yours, Dani Halstead. Every bit as good as yours. And possibly—" the blue eyes bored into hers "—a lot better."

The challenge to her honesty was like a punch to the heart. Dani stared at him, fiercely justifying her stance with him to herself. Yes, he was attractive. More attractive than any other man she had met. Probably more attractive than any man she would ever meet. She had spent a wonderful day with him and she did like him. Enormously.

She wanted to have more time with him, time to know him better, time to feel her way with him and find out if they had a future. He was handing her that opportunity. But what motive did he have? He couldn't be considering anything lasting between them, could he? Why would he? She was no match for him.

He leaned forward, reached across the table and took one of her hands in his. His fingers stroked across her wrist, softly, seductively, persuasively. "Give it a chance, Dani. That's all I'm asking."

In his eyes was the promise of the rightness she had felt with him last night, the promise of all the possibilities in the world between them. But was it a deception? An illusion? A mirage conjured up by her own secret desires?

Dani's body rebelled against the caution in her mind. Her heart pumped a wild *yes*. Her stomach melted with compliance. Her legs denied any strength to walk away. Her lungs refused to breathe properly until she was prepared to consider surrender.

"I'll think about it," she managed huskily.

"Tomorrow," he pressed.

"All right. I'll give you an answer tomorrow. After I've done Mrs. B's cleaning."

"What time will you be home?"

"Five o'clock."

"I'll be there."

He released her hand and sat back, emanating a supreme confidence that he would win his way with her. Dani didn't know if she cared any more if he did. There was a time in life when it was necessary to throw caution to the wind. Perhaps this was the time for her.

And who knew? Maybe the way to a man's heart was through his stomach!

CHAPTER SEVEN

THE NEXT MORNING Dani found out that Mrs. B didn't need her as a stand-in cleaner any more. She had contacted a professional cleaning service, which assured her they could take over her run permanently, and she was about to recommend it to her gentlemen. Mrs. B had decided she was never going to do cleaning again. Except for Henry, of course. Mrs. B was moving out to a new life. No more loneliness for her. From now on it was going to be Hilda and Henry together in his Woollhara home.

Which left Dani with a great hole in her life. Her one close friend was deserting her for a man. Not that she minded about Mrs. B settling in with Henry Newbold. She was happy for her. But with no-one nearby to talk to, it did mean a lot of lonely days and nights stretching ahead of her.

As it was, she was unexpectedly free for the day, with a heavy decision hanging on her mind. It wasn't that she didn't know what she wanted to do. That was not in question. She simply didn't understand what Cameron McFarlane saw in her, apart from her first-class cooking. Dani didn't like walking into a situation she didn't understand. It made her feel out of control.

Despite all the disappointments and disasters Dani had weathered over the years, she never felt she couldn't control her life. Occasionally she made judgements and decisions that didn't work out properly, but that was to be expected. Everybody did that. It happened more frequently to her because luck was definitely against her.

Nevertheless, she always picked herself up and moved on, she hoped steering a wiser course into the future. The problem with Cameron McFarlane was that she had more than a sneaking suspicion that to become his personal live-in chef had a few consequences. However much she wanted to be with him, it appeared to be the height of folly rather than a rational, sensible decision with a happy ending.

Yet Mrs. B's good opinion of Cameron kept playing around in her mind, teasing her into a different perception of his character. Mrs. B had been delighted she and Cameron had got on so well that he had wanted to spend all yesterday with her.

"Such a kind man. I really shall miss doing for him. All the treats he's given me . . ." She smiled with fond remembrance. "But it will be nicer sharing with Henry."

"What treats, Mrs. B?" Dani questioned.

"Oh, there was always food he didn't want because he'd be away. And complimentary tickets to the movies. Every time I mentioned a movie I'd like to see, somehow someone gave him a ticket to it that he didn't have time to use and he'd give it to me." Her brown eyes twinkled brightly in delighted anticipation of a happy outcome to another romance. "He's a good man, Dani. The kind who'd really look after you. You do like him, don't you?''

Dani's agreement had made Mrs. B look extremely satisfied, as though everything was neatly settled in her mind. Not so in Dani's. Yet she was forced to continue revising her judgement of Cameron McFarlane. He hadn't been conning Mrs. B with his charm. He had given at least as much as Mrs. B had given him. Possibly more. She remembered his readiness to oblige in sending Mrs. B flowers and felt ashamed of her cynicism.

Maybe he did have a good heart. She couldn't doubt he was generous. Maybe he had no bad motives at all. Was it possible he was totally sincere in all he'd said to her?

Since the wisest person she knew was her grandmother, Dani figured that her free day could be fruitfully employed talking a few things over with her. She could not, of course, spell out the details, but a general overview of things could very well clear up a few murky areas in her brain. Dani wanted to have all her wits about her, her facts absolutely straight and a sensible decision under her belt when Cameron McFarlane came for her this afternoon.

A telephone call ensured that a visit was more than welcome, and Dani set off, her spirits automatically lifting as she took the train that her grandmother would meet at Camden, on the south-western outskirts of the city. Dani loved going to Grandma's place.

Nicole had hated their holidays there, always complaining there was nothing to do. But that was mainly because Nicole recoiled from getting her hands and clothes dirty. Nicole had never known how to have fun and probably never would. Which was a pity. It was one of the few times that Dani didn't envy Nicole—in fact, felt a stab of sympathy for her.

Dani wanted to talk to Grandma about Nicole. It was not something she had done before, because most of the time she wanted to forget Nicole. Dani had made up her mind that she believed Cameron's assertion about not having any intimate association with her sister, but she wanted a clearer understanding of Nicole's motives for saying what she had said.

She hoped Grandma had some useful insights because Dani wanted to smooth things over between herself and her sister. After all, Christmas was Christmas, they were family, and that particular day was hurtling towards her like an express train.

Time seemed to slip by very quickly and suddenly the train was pulling in at Camden. Dani hurried off and raced out of the station to where she knew her grandmother would be waiting. She grinned at the spritely white-haired lady who waved to her from beside the blue pick-up truck she had been driving for the last twenty years.

Her grandmother's wild mop of curls was cropped short for practicality, and she wore her "town clothes," which were always pink. On this occasion they were candy-striped cotton slacks and a matching overblouse.

They hugged and kissed, and Dani was quite sure if she hadn't seen Grandma for ten years instead of two weeks, the warmth and affection of the greeting would be the same. Grandma was unflappable.

They piled into the truck for the twenty-minute trip out to the farm. No comment was made about Dani's visit on a Monday, since Monday was her usual day off work anyhow, and Dani prompted her grandmother into telling all her news.

One of the dogs had a new litter of pups, and the rooster in the henhouse had given the alarm that a fox was about. He was a feisty bird, well worth his keep. He knew how to protect his hens. There was certainly a place for such roosters, Dani thought, and wondered if Cameron McFarlane would ever care enough about her to be protective.

When they reached the farm, Grandma and Dani did the rounds of the animals, then with all due greetings made, they settled at the table in the huge country kitchen, which was Grandma's domain. Over a cup of tea and Grandma's pumpkin scones, the old lady regarded her grand-daughter with shrewd probing brown eyes.

"So what's wrong, Dani?" she asked quietly. "Why have you come to visit me today?"

Dani heaved a rueful sigh. Nothing got past Grandma. She could spot a lie coming a mile off, and if any mischief had been done behind her back, somehow she always knew about that, too. She explained it away by saying the birds told her, but Dani figured she had some sixth sense.

"I'm trying to work something out, Grandma," she started hesitantly.

"Fine," her grandmother encouraged. She moved down to the far end of the table, where her tapestry frame was set out on a special cloth. She threaded a needle with one of the coloured wools, gave Dani her listening smile and started stitching away.

This is it, Dani thought. The big one. It wasn't a time for half-measures. She had to go in boots and all. "It's about a man, Grandma."

"Fine," said Grandma non-committally.

Dani took a deep breath. "Nicole told me something about him—" impossible to specify what "—but I don't think it was true."

Grandma looked up. "Why don't you think it's true, Dani?" she asked quietly.

Dani paused for reflection. Why didn't she believe Nicole? It certainly suited her purpose not to believe her. But it went deeper than that.

"It doesn't *feel* right, Grandma."

It was as simple as that, really. All the vibrations she was getting from Nicole and Cameron McFarlane... they didn't fit together. Someone was lying, and all her instincts said it was Nicole.

"Then perhaps Nicole is lying," Grandma said quietly. Her stitching never altered a beat. Calm, unflappable, imperturbable.

"But why, Grandma? Why should Nicole tell such a dreadful lie?"

Grandma looked up at her. "There could be a lot of reasons, Dani."

"Such as?"

"Perhaps Nicole is jealous of you. Perhaps she envies what you could have."

"Ha!" said Dani with derisive scorn. "Nicole, jealous of me? Fat chance, Grandma! Nicole is the one who has everything. She's—"

"Has she, Dani? Has she got everything?"

She didn't have Cameron McFarlane, Dani thought, and Cameron had also suggested Nicole might be jealous of her. That had to be the answer, Dani decided. Nicole had wanted Cameron and she hated the thought that he preferred her younger sister. Although Heaven alone knew why he did!

"Nicole is beautiful, Grandma. She's brainy—"

"Do you think that's so important, Dani?"

That stopped Dani in her tracks. Only yesterday she had made the same point to Cameron McFarlane, listing his on-show attributes and telling him they weren't the most important things, that they weren't enough for her when it came right down to the nitty-gritty. But would men think the same way about Nicole? The evidence was overwhelmingly against it.

"Well, they're assets most people would like to have, Grandma," she defended.

Her grandmother made no reply. For long minutes Dani watched her carry on with her stitching, her hands moving rhythmically and methodically in their repetitive task. Dani loved Grandma's hands. They were old and gnarled and weather-beaten from farm work, oversized for a woman, but they were the tenderest, most comforting hands in the world.

They had consoled and soothed her when she was hurt, bathed her forehead when she had a childhood fever, gently delivered all kinds of animals. They were capable, loving hands. Dani hoped that when she grew old, she would have loving hands like that for her grandchildren.

Suddenly the shrewd brown eyes snapped up and looked quizzically at her. "Do you really, Dani? Do you really want that?"

Which left Dani bewildered. "Want what, Grandma?"

"To be like Nicole."

The thought flabbergasted Dani. She had sometimes wondered what it would be like, but to be actually like Nicole . . .

"Certainly not, Grandma. No way! I'd much rather be me."

Grandma gave a self-satisfied little smile as she went back to her stitching.

"There is one other thing, Grandma . . ."

"I'm all ears," Grandma encouraged.

"It's a man."

"The same man?"

"Yes."

"Well?"

Dani blurted it out. "I don't understand why he's attracted to me."

Grandma looked up. "Don't you think you're attractive, Dani?"

"Well, yes, but I'm not Nicole." Or Simone, either, she thought.

"Beauty," said Grandma portentously, "is in the eye of the beholder."

Dani was disappointed. She had expected more from Grandma than that. Dani didn't see how she could base her life on such a dubious proposition. It simply didn't have the same ring of truth about it as "disasters come in threes" or "the early bird catches the worm." She suspected it was in the same vein as "the way to a man's heart is through his stomach," which had yet to be verified in Dani's experience.

"Well, Grandma, would you like me to make us some lunch?"

She started to rise, but Grandma said, "Sit down, Dani. I think I have to tell you a story." She gave Dani her sweet imperturbable smile that seemed to embrace a great experience and knowledge of the world.

Dani sat. There was more to come. Maybe she would still get some light thrown onto her problem, some wise advice that would illuminate the path and the darkness ahead.

Grandma sat back complacently, taking her time. Grandma was never hurried in anything she did. "It's a fairy story," she began, and resumed her stitching. "But for all it's a fairy story, it's true enough." She glanced up momentarily. "See what you can make of it, if anything at all."

Dani waited.

"Once upon a time, a long time ago, there was a young girl. She was pretty enough, and attractive enough, but she had one glaring fault."

Dani had a prickling sensation that she knew what was coming. She didn't like it. Not one bit.

"The fault in the girl was grotesque. She was always conscious of it and tried to hide it." Grandma took one long pull of the tapestry wool so her arm was extended to its fullest extent. "You see, Dani, this girl had very huge, ugly hands. She tried her best to keep them out of sight. She put them behind her back. She sat on them. Mealtimes were a terrible torture because they exposed her hands to everyone's critical view."

"I wouldn't think like that, Grandma," Dani interjected defensively.

"Of course not, my dear. Anyway, this little girl grew up and one day she fell in love with a man." Grandma smiled an inner solitary smile. "Very much in love," she said firmly. "One day this man asked her to marry him. And do you know what this silly girl did?"

Dani shook her head. Her throat had gone dry. She had no idea what was coming next.

"Well, this silly girl," Grandma continued, "said to the man, 'How can you love me when I've got such ugly hands?' She then held her hands up in front of his face to prove her point. Oh, she was such a silly girl then."

"What happened?" Dani croaked.

"Fortunately for the girl, the man she loved was a very sensible man. He didn't tell a lie and say to her that she had the prettiest hands in the world. No, what he did was quite different. He looked her firmly in the eyes and said, 'If you love me, you'll forget you ever said that to me, as I'm going to forget you ever said it. Otherwise every time I see your hands I'll think how ugly they are. I love *you*. Not your hands. Between us, I never want your hands to be mentioned again, not in all our married life. If you don't keep to that, they'll become a stupid issue, and someday dreadful wounding words will be spoken that will never be forgiven.' And the girl, at last, got some sense and promised him she would never mention her hands again or let them get in the way.''

Grandma stuck her needle into the side of her tapestry with the air of having finished all she wanted to say. She sat and gazed contentedly through the kitchen window, looking out over the long back yard with her animals and vegetable garden. Her domain.

Dani felt she had got the point. It didn't do any good to let shortcomings get in the way of something that could mean an awful lot to you. In fact, Dani made an instant resolution never to think about her freckles again. She wasn't going to throw Nicole in Cameron's face again, either.

Dani cleared her throat and spoke her heart. ''I love your hands, Grandma.''

''So do I, my dear,'' she answered softly.

''Hands were never mentioned again, Grandma?'' Dani hated asking, but she needed to know.

''Only once,'' Grandma said. ''Only once.'' A smile lit her face, a smile of serene inner satisfaction and contentment, a radiance of benign appeal.

''What happened?''

''Oh, a very rude man once made an unseemly remark...''

''And?''

''Your grandfather had a lot of Irish in him, Dani. He really believed in the things he believed in. He hit the man once—what a blow it was!—straight between the teeth. The man went down like a lead balloon. Blood everywhere. He didn't bother getting to his feet.''

Dani looked at her grandmother in shock. Here was a woman who wouldn't hurt a fly, who went out of her way to give compassion and support to those who suffered, but her face was suffused with supreme pleasure in the painful blow that had been struck on her behalf. It was clear that she had drifted off into another world, a world of dreams where love blossomed and grew in richness and strength, and there had been happiness and laughter and tears. Another world, which was still very real and vivid to her.

Dani didn't interrupt her reverie. She understood precisely what Grandma was saying.

What are defects to you might not be defects to others...unless you let them get in the way. If you were confident in yourself, no-one noticed. If you weren't confident, then it would automatically get in the way.

When it came to real love, superficial things like that simply didn't matter. The word *love* gave Dani a pleasant little tingle along her spine. Was she in love with Cameron McFarlane? Could anyone fall in love that quickly?

A strong sense of decision swept through her. She was going to see this feeling through, whatever the truth and the consequences. She had to take the chance that everything might turn out right.

Time slipped by. Dani made lunch for her grandmother who seemed content to sit dreaming of other times. But Dani had to get herself organized. She had another appointment today. Her mind was made up, and she was ready to act on her decisions.

She rose from her chair, knelt beside her grandmother and placed her head upon the loving hands so carefully folded together on her lap. "I love you, Grandma."

One hand slid away and lifted to caress Dani's tangled brown curls. "I love you, too, Dani."

A most satisfying visit, Dani thought, as they made the trip to Camden station. She felt there had been a new and significant development in her relationship with Grandma. More adult... more something... she didn't know what.

But she certainly understood Grandma much better now. She wondered what she would do if Grandma died. She realised it was inevitable, and what would happen was that she would have her own children, and they would have their children, and if everything worked out right, one day she would become just like Grandma and be wise and able to help people.

Dani gave her grandmother an extra big hug at the railway station, but it was Grandma's words that arrested her. "I'll look forward to meeting your man on Christmas Day, Dani," she said simply, but there was a knowing twinkle in her eyes.

On the train journey into the city, Dani pondered those words and their significance. Damn Nicole! she thought. Dani had to live her own life. She had found her wings and she was going to fly and soar into the unknown, into a new life. And when Christmas Day came, if Cameron wanted to be with her at her family home, she would be proud to take him to meet Grandma.

Dani could hardly wait for five o'clock.

And Cameron McFarlane.

CHAPTER EIGHT

CONSCIOUS OF TIME ticking away, Dani whizzed around her flat, packing all the things she needed to take with her. She carried a box of perishable food to the top flat and left it outside the quarrelling couple's door. When she was satisfied that she had everything organized, she set to work on her appearance.

She washed and blow-dried her troublesome hair. If Cameron thought her hair beautiful, she wasn't going to hide it in a plait. It ended up rather like a wild halo of crinkles and curls around her face, but at least it was a shiny brown. And if she took away the freckles across her nose and cheekbones, there wasn't much wrong with her face.

Cameron had said she had a saucy mouth that begged to be kissed. Her nose wasn't perfect but she didn't mind the little tilt at the end. As for her eyes, well, hazel could be more interesting than plain green or brown, and she did have thick curly lashes. From now on she was going to think positive.

For good measure, she put on the clothes she had bought for Christmas Day. The well-tailored white slacks and the boldly striped red and white jersey top were really quite striking on her, Dani thought. One thing she did have was a well-proportioned figure.

Cameron thought so, too, or he wouldn't have stared at her in her yellow maillot.

Dani worked herself up into feeling absolutely great about herself by the time Cameron called for her at precisely five o'clock. Then, despite all her marvellous resolutions, she took one look at him and her new-found confidence cracked. He wore a light grey business suit that not only emphasised the striking features of the man, but impressed on her that he could take his place in any circle he chose and be the centre of it. He emanated a self-assurance that no-one could take away from him, while Dani felt herself deflating like a pricked balloon.

Nevertheless, he was here for her, and at least she was a damned good cook, Dani argued fiercely to herself. She would make him appreciate that, if nothing else. Her eyes challenged his with tigerish pride.

"We haven't talked wages yet," she said, stubbornly determined on making him respect her professionally and not take anything for granted.

Cameron named a daily rate that was more than Dani had earned in her life. And for considerably less work. She swallowed three times to counteract the tremulous upheaval it caused inside her. So much money could only mean that Cameron was very intent on having her. She desperately hoped he didn't think he was buying more than her expertise in the kitchen. Her love, her body, her feelings were not for sale. Or maybe he thought . . .

"If that's meant to cover house cleaning as well, you can forget it, Cameron," she asserted. "Mrs. B has undoubtedly informed you that she won't be cleaning your house any more. And neither will I. House cleaning is not my vocation in life. I was only helping out a friend."

Another thought struck her before he could reply. "I should also tell you that I don't believe in double standards when it comes to housework. Or in any other area. As far as living in the same house is concerned, you pick up after you, and I'll pick up after me."

"I've already contracted the cleaning service Mrs. B recommended to do that work, Dani," he assured her, amusement dancing in his eyes. "Your job is to be my personal chef. Nothing more, nothing less."

"That's all right, then. I don't want you to have any false expectations."

"How could I with you?"

Dani didn't like the sound of that. Maybe he had lost interest in wanting her. She frowned at the way his mouth was quirking. "What's that supposed to mean?" she demanded.

The quirking stretched into a wide grin. "Dani, you lay everything straight on the line. Which I like, I might add. It's a most refreshing change from the usual artifice that most young women employ."

Dani's heart gave a pleasurable little skip. He liked her for being the way she was. Maybe Grandma was right after all, and Cameron found nothing wrong with her. She gave him a brilliant smile. Her bright hazel eyes sparkled loving approval at him.

It seemed to cause his grin to falter. A strange look flitted over his face, as though he had suddenly been struck by some new thought. He was staring at her, but his eyes had the glazed expression of being inwardly focussed. It played havoc with Dani's stomach. Then, whatever it was, he snapped out of it and leaned down to pick up the packed suitcase that stood by the door.

"Let's go," he said.

Dani had a strong premonition of the hand of fate as she locked up her flat and followed Cameron to his car. They were going off together, going to be together day in and day out. Maybe she would never come back to live in the old terrace house. Just like Mrs. B.

"I haven't bought any food for dinner tonight," she said as Cameron drove them towards his home.

"I did." He flashed her a smile. "You can take over the buying tomorrow. Then you can keep surprising me."

She laughed out of sheer nervous excitement. "Have you any definite dislikes that I shouldn't cook, Cameron?"

"Tripe. I hate tripe. And liver. Nothing with liver. I'm a very plain eater." His eyes sparkled at her. "I'm looking forward to being educated to higher and better things by one of the world's leading experts."

"I'll balance plain with fancy. That way you're guaranteed something you can enjoy as well as something you can try."

"Precisely my formula for life."

Dani didn't know if she approved of that or not. She had a keen admiration for the mind of Cameron McFarlane, but his heart was still very much a mystery to her. She hoped that in time it would be revealed to her.

When they arrived at the house in Double Bay, Cameron carried her suitcase to the guest bedroom suite she had used before. "Take your time unpacking," he invited. "There's no hurry to get to the kitchen. I'm happy to eat when you're ready."

She favoured him with another brilliant smile for being so nice and obliging. Cameron's gaze fastened on her mouth for several heart-kicking seconds, then swept to her feet before slowly lifting to her eyes again. "I have a house rule, too," he said.

"Oh?" Dani choked out.

"No chef's uniform." He smiled. "I like what you're wearing much better."

Dani could feel her whole body flushing with pleasure. "What about when you have guests?" she asked.

"Then you will be the hostess as well as the chef."

Dani was filled with delight that he wanted her at his side amongst his smart friends and associates. There was only one problem. "I may not have appropriate clothes for that, Cameron."

"Then it will be my pleasure to find and purchase the appropriate clothes for you to wear."

Dani took a deep breath. This was tricky ground. She wasn't sure she should find it acceptable, but the thought of having clothes that Cameron wanted to see her in was very seductive. Something very female inside her insisted any protest was stupid.

Cameron's gaze wandered down to the rise and fall of her breasts, lingered a moment, then flicked up again. "Definitely a pleasure," he said with another smile. "You have a perfect body, Dani."

Beautiful hair, perfect body, and he liked her being straight with him. Dani's cup of happiness was flowing over like a fountain.

It was only after he left her to her unpacking that she cautioned herself about his intentions towards her. Getting her into bed with him was one of them. Cameron had made no bones about that. But he had more or less promised not to pounce. Freedom of choice, he had said. But if she didn't choose when he wanted her to, what then?

Dani did her best to shrug off the question. She was here with him now. No point in crossing bridges until she came to them. Maybe she could alter the courses of those bridges anyway. She was not without some power, since he wanted her. She also had the will to fight for what she wanted.

When Cameron joined her in the kitchen, Dani had already planned the menu for dinner. He had changed into casual clothes, and Dani was somewhat distracted from her preparations for a while. His jeans made her very aware of his extremely virile masculinity, and he hadn't bothered doing up all the buttons on his white sports shirt, which left a deep V of smoothly tanned chest. Dani wondered if it was deliberate enticement for her to touch him there as she had the other night.

Yet he talked to her in a perfectly natural manner, and Dani's inner tension gradually eased away in the pleasure of his company. She braised lobster medallions in white wine and served them with a salad. She cooked steaks on the barbecue, having already popped a cheese and potato dish into the oven. She accompanied this with snow peas and honeyed carrot sticks. Finally she produced perfectly baked pears with a fresh strawberry sauce and ice-cream.

Cameron was full of appreciation. Dani glowed more approval at him. When she brought up the subject of food expenses, he said she could break the bank for all he cared, so long as she kept giving him meals as marvellous as that. She had an absolute free hand to buy whatever she liked. He would meet all bills with pleasure.

Dani was beginning to think there might be a lot of truth in the saying, "the way to a man's heart is through his stomach." If his stomach was properly satisfied, it probably softened up his heart for easier entry. Anyhow, it seemed like a good idea to test this theory and see if Cameron would open up to her.

Having cleaned up the kitchen, Dani took their after-dinner coffee into the living room where Cameron was lazily stretched out on one of his leather armchairs looking supremely content. She was conscious of his eyes glittering over her in an excitingly possessive way as she sat on the chair beside his. Dani had to compose her mind before introducing the subject she wanted to talk about.

"I've told you practically all about myself, Cameron," she pointed out. "I'd like to know more about you."

He gave her an indulgent smile. "What do you want to know, Dani?"

"About your childhood."

The smile turned into a grimace. "I prefer to forget that."

"Why?" She wasn't going to let him evade her questions tonight.

He flashed her a sardonic look. "I'm not confused about my sexuality, Dani."

She flushed at the reminder of her provocative suggestion.

He grinned at her embarrassment. "Nor do I believe I'm overly self-centred or fussy. I simply know what I want and don't want. And I don't want you psychoanalysing my childhood and coming up with the wrong answers."

"Then tell me the right answers," she argued reasonably.

"The right answers are that I learnt the right lessons, and I don't intend to make the mistakes first-hand experience taught me were destructive," he answered dryly.

"Like what?" she persisted. "What harm can it do to tell me about it if your family are all gone?"

"They're not all gone. I simply disowned them," he stated matter-of-factly.

Dani stared at him in shock. "You disowned them?"

"It was better for them. Better for me." His eyes softly mocked as he added, "Life is not always the straight line you want it to be, Dani."

"How is it *better?*" she demanded.

"My father has a family. My mother has a family. Both are separate from the other. My parents are much happier not to be reminded that they were once married to each other.''

The child of a divorce, and a bitter one, Dani guessed. ''But what about you? Don't they care for you?''

''I embarrass them.''

''Why?''

''Because I know too much about them. I know what they want to forget.''

''Like what?''

He gave her a twisted little smile. ''Dani, people don't like to be faced with their uglier side. My parents were not into parenting when they were married to each other. Their marriage was a battle ground. Robbie and I were merely weapons they hurled at each other. When they divorced, Mother got custody and quickly shoved us into boarding school so she could get on with her love-life, and my father got loaded with exorbitant fees. Mother was a winner. She liked to win everything. Sending Robbie and me to boarding school was a complete win for her.''

No loving at all, Dani thought sadly. She was no longer surprised that he shied clear of marriage if that was his childhood experience of it. But what of his brother or sister? ''Robbie?'' she asked.

He winced. ''My younger brother.''

''Where is he now?''

Cameron's face took on a shuttered look. ''He drowned when I was fifteen. It happened the day after his thirteenth birthday.''

His jaw tightened. A muscle in his cheek contracted. His hands, which had lain relaxed on the armrests of the leather chair, curled into knuckle-white fists as though he wanted to hit out at the fate that had taken his brother from him.

Dani hesitated to intrude on a grief that still had the power to pulse through him with such angry violence, yet she felt it might do him good to talk about it instead of keeping it bottled up inside him. "How did it happen?" she asked softly.

He flashed her a look that was both haunted and resentful before he tempered it to flat derision. "We were spending our obligatory time with Father during school vacation. We went fishing. A storm came up suddenly. The boat was capsized by a wave. It was late evening. We hung on to the boat. No-one came looking for us. Night fell. Robbie got tired. A large wave crashed into us and he slipped off. Off into the darkness. I couldn't find him. I searched for hours. He never came back."

Flat, toneless, as if somehow he had failed. No appreciation of the strength and courage he'd shown.

"What happened to you?" Dani asked, wanting to draw him out of the past and back to her.

His mouth twisted as though he hated his own survival. "The next morning I was found by a fisherman."

She wanted to say, "I'm sorry, Cameron. I'm sure you tried the best you could," but that wasn't the best way to show caring and compassion. Touching was better than words. Grandma had shown her that. So she reached out and gently covered his closed fist with her hand, her fingers softly stroking until his hand relaxed under hers.

His eyes regarded her quizzically for several long moments before he spoke. "I'm glad you didn't say anything. No false sympathy."

"There are no words for what you've endured, Cameron," she said quietly.

His fingers slowly and deliberately linked with hers, giving a tactile acceptance to an empathy he had neither invited nor expected, but which was there... the beginning of true closeness between them, a lowering of barriers.

"You know what I hated most?" he said, his mind still dwelling on the past.

She shook her head.

"My parents attending Robbie's funeral. Supposedly mourning their son." His voice carried a dark mockery as he added, "They fought over him... even there."

Like the couple in the upstairs flat, Dani thought. "I understand," she whispered. "In a way I've heard it all before. I don't want it to happen to me."

"Nor me."

They sat together holding hands, enjoying togetherness in their mutual thoughts. Dani wondered if Cameron had too deep-rooted a prejudice against marriage to ever consider it. Yet staying alone and single and having the occasional affair wasn't the way to handle life and get the best out of it. Life was about loving. Loving was about life. Dani was sure of it.

"I've never told anyone about that before," he mused, more to himself than to her.

Dani wondered if it was some revelation to him that he had opened up to her. She couldn't help feeling uniquely privileged. It had to mean he trusted her with his confidence. Perhaps it meant even more than that, she thought hopefully.

"You don't see your parents any more?" she asked.

He shook his head. "That stopped after I started publishing. Psychology sweeps the human soul bare. My parents tend to take my books personally. I must admit my experience with them did give me the desire to know why people are the way they are. Why they do what they do. How people make their own worlds. A search for reasons. A search for solutions."

"What solutions have you found?"

Any brooding darkness in his soul was banished as he smiled at her. His blue eyes danced teasingly as he repeated the very words she had spoken to him yesterday. "That having a good heart, kindness, honesty, loyalty, fidelity... things like that... will get you through most problems."

Then he lifted their linked hands to his mouth and brushed his lips over her knuckles. Dani's heart jolted.

"Even better if you mix all that with some loving," he murmured, his eyes warming to more than teasing.

"I think it's time I said goodnight, Cameron," Dani managed to force out.

He kissed her hand again, his eyes steady on hers, watching, wanting. "Are you sure about that, Dani?" he asked softly.

"Yes." Her throat felt so constricted it was barely a whisper. She swallowed hard then added, "Thank you for talking to me."

He sighed and gave her a whimsical little smile as he released her hand. "My pleasure. I hope you sleep well."

"And you," she said, willing strength into her shaky legs as she stood up.

She was extremely conscious of him watching her as she left the living room. Her skin tingled all over, and the back of her neck positively prickled. *It is too soon,* Dani kept reciting to herself. *Far too soon.* But she didn't let herself think about what it was too soon for until she was safely in bed with the lights out.

What would it mean to Cameron?

Dani knew what it would mean to her.

And if it was the beginning of the end, she would shrivel up inside for evermore.

CHAPTER NINE

THE NEXT MORNING Dani made up menus for the rest
of the week and wrote a shopping list to cover everything. Cameron insisted on accompanying her to the
markets, saying it would be a new experience for him.
Dani was only too happy to spend the whole day with
him.

It was fun shopping together. Cameron waggled his
eyebrows over some of her choices, but she challenged him to wait and taste. He seemed blithely un-
concerned about the cost of anything, even adding a
few very extravagant items to her shopping list. Like
black cherries, which were obscenely expensive.

"I like cherries," he said, popping one into his
mouth and eating it with a blissful look on his face.
His eyes twinkled with teasing devilment. "Of course
there is one thing I'd like better..."

Dani declined to ask. He had already informed her
that oysters were well known for their aphrodisiac
properties, were very healthy, and they should both eat
plenty of them. With an air of complete innocence, he
stocked up on French champagne, extolling its qualities and the delightful way it bubbled through one's
head. Dani couldn't help laughing at his good-
humoured suggestiveness, and the way his eyes made

love to her, had her heart in a constant state of barely repressible exhilaration.

But while Cameron was certainly an expert and exciting player at love, Dani still wasn't sure that *his* heart was involved. In her need to know and understand him, she decided she should waste no time in reading up on how he thought in the books he had written. She waited until dinner was over that night, then asked Cameron if she could borrow one of his books from the study.

"Not one of mine, Dani."

"But I wanted . . ."

The blue eyes were suddenly very hard and serious. "No. Any other book. I don't want you reading mine."

Dani felt bewildered. "Why not?"

"Because those books weren't written for you."

Still she didn't understand his objection. "I know that, Cameron, but I might learn something about you from them."

"No. There's nothing for you to learn from them, Dani. You're far better off the way you are."

"What do you mean . . . the way I am?"

His mouth curled into an ironic little smile. "Not screwed up. You've got a straight line in your head, Dani. It's a *good* straight line. Believe me. I know. And I wouldn't want anything to mess up that straight line."

She challenged him. "Do you think I'm a simpleton, Cameron? That I can't read things and sort out what's right or wrong for me?"

"No. But when I make love to you, I don't want you thinking you should be doing anything that doesn't come naturally to you." His eyes took on a gleam of sheer animal wickedness. "You can learn far more about me that way. Much more enthralling than taking one of my books to bed with you."

Was it all sex with him? Dani worried. Nothing else? "I think I'll stick to a book tonight," she said, and took herself off to the study, out of Cameron's firing range.

THE NEXT MORNING he announced he had invited a number of people for dinner on Thursday night so they had to spend today shopping for an appropriate hostess outfit for her. He did not want her to feel pressured for time tomorrow.

"How many people?" Dani demanded. "You should have told me yesterday when we were buying food."

"Only eight including us. And it doesn't have to be anything special, Dani. I want you at the table with me, not in the kitchen. So, if you can prepare everything beforehand..."

"Last time you told me twenty and it ended up forty," Dani reminded him pointedly.

"That was a party. Who can control a party?" he contended. "This is a sit-down dinner. No gatecrashers, I promise."

"Are you absolutely sure of that, Cameron?" she asked suspiciously.

"I give you my word." His eyes twinkled at her. "Which I have amply proved to you so far."

Dani had to concede he had been as good as his word, even against his inclinations. She smiled. "Okay."

"Right! So we go shopping for clothes. There are some fine boutiques at the Double Bay centre."

"They'd be dreadfully expensive, Cameron," Dani quickly warned. The Double Bay centre was well-known for its luxury boutiques, catering to the tastes of the wealthy who lived in the area.

"Dani, I am not concerned about money. We get what I think is appropriate," he declared with decisive finality.

Dani found out that what Cameron thought appropriate was absolutely out of this world. It was made of silk chiffon, printed in a glorious array of colours, a rich vibrant green, royal blue and purple, but predominantly bright yellow and orange. The flowers on the bodice were beaded to emphasise the colours and make them sparkle brilliantly. A wide band of black, elasticised to cling to the curve of her waist and hips, separated the bodice from the skirt. The latter consisted of three layers of chiffon, falling to different lengths in a cascade of handkerchief points. It was a skirt that made Dani want to twirl around and dance. She couldn't resist a couple of twirls when she paraded the dress for Cameron's approval. It was the most beautiful, the most feminine, the most stunning dress Dani had ever seen, let alone worn.

"Perfect!" Cameron declared, his eyes laughing at her as though he knew exactly how she felt.

There was only one drawback. She couldn't wear a bra with it. The back of the bodice plunged in a deep cowl that dipped right to the waistline. Who cares, she thought. The dress was working some magic on her. She felt beautiful in it. Beautiful and sexy and deliciously wicked. And it felt good to feel that way. Particularly with Cameron looking at her as though she was all he could ever want in a woman.

He insisted on buying a black beaded evening bag that went with the dress, and then, of course, they had to get the right shoes. Nothing but a Christian Dior pair in black and gold would do.

"This has to be costing you a fortune, Cameron," Dani whispered guiltily.

"I'll write another best-seller," he insisted.

Dani simply couldn't argue. She had never believed she could ever look striking, but she could. She really could in the dress Cameron had bought her. And a million stars were popping off in her head. What was money compared to that feeling? Even if it was only a once-in-a-lifetime feeling, it was worth it. And she loved Cameron for giving it to her.

Of course she loved him for other reasons, too. All of them were bubbling inside her as they took their marvellous purchases home.

"Happy?" Cameron asked.

She laughed. "I suppose it's mad to be happy about a dress . . ."

"No. It's good to be happy, Dani. And it makes me feel good to see your eyes sparkling like a Christmas tree." He slanted a wry little smile at her. "I'm tempted to take advantage of it, but I won't. This isn't an attempt to put pressure on you."

"You couldn't, even if you wanted to, Cameron," Dani said with utter certainty.

He laughed softly to himself, then shot her a twinkling look of approval. "I prefer you to choose."

That was fine by Dani. She hoped that when it came time to choose, Cameron would have more on his mind than immediate gratification.

For the rest of the day, Dani felt there was a new closeness between them . . . a warmer understanding, an intimacy of feeling, a deep happiness in being together. When she went to bed that night she wished she was not alone. She craved the sense of togetherness they had been sharing. She missed it.

Dani was up bright and early the next morning, excited about being with Cameron again, excited about tonight's dinner party, when she would wear the dress for him. She was brimming with the joy of life as she bustled around, getting Cameron's breakfast ready. When he came into the kitchen he looked happy, too. He smiled as much as she did, and every time their eyes met it was with warm pleasure. Dani felt like dancing or shouting from sheer happiness.

Later on in the morning they had a swim together and Dani was towelling herself dry when she heard the telephone ringing in the kitchen. She called out to Cameron who was still swimming his daily fifty laps, and he called back for her to answer it until he could get there. Dani had no concern about doing so. It was a perfectly reasonable request.

"Cameron McFarlane's residence," she announced into the receiver.

Silence.

"Who's calling, please?" Dani inquired pleasantly.

"You're the chef who was there last Saturday night, aren't you?" came an accusing female voice.

Dani instantly bridled. What woman from the party was calling Cameron? And why? "Yes, I am. Cameron is in the pool. He'll be here in a minute," she explained coolly. "If you would please hold on..."

"Well, I'm glad to know you're human," came the acid comment.

"What makes you think that?" Dani demanded, highly suspicious of the remark.

"I spoke to you, remember? Simone. Simone Lessing."

"Oh, yes!" Dani affected surprise over her inner dismay. She didn't care for the idea of Simone ringing Cameron. Not one bit!

"So you decided it might not be so bad to keep on bedding Cameron, after all," Simone taunted.

Dani dragged in a deep breath. "Simone, Cameron told me you were a very smart lady. Really clever. Doing your doctorate at the university. Among other things. He also thinks you're a very nice person. I'm sure you must be or he wouldn't have spent so much time with you."

Dani paused for the other woman to take stock of her niceness. Then she delivered the punch line. "What I can't understand is how you could think of him as nothing but a stud. Cameron is much more than a great male body, and if you—"

"Thank you, Dani," said his quiet voice behind her.

She swung around to meet eyes that seared hers with questions. All of them uncomfortable. But she had to defend him, didn't she? Simone deserved the feminine equivalent of a knuckle sandwich for thinking about him the way she did.

Cameron took the receiver out of her hand, his eyes still burning into her as he spoke into it. "I apologise for keeping you waiting, Simone. What can I do for you?"

Sheer black jealousy swept through Dani. She turned her back on Cameron and his conversation with his all too recent lover and marched over to the kitchen sink. She turned on the cold water and started washing the grapes she had left there. She heard Cameron say yes, no, thank you, then the click of the receiver being hung up.

"What was that all about, Dani?" he asked quietly.

Grapes were dropping off the bunch everywhere, but Dani didn't notice. She kept on washing as she bit her reply out through fiercely clenched teeth.

"I thought you didn't like being regarded as a womaniser."

"I don't."

"So how come you were dumb enough to go to bed with a woman who thinks that?"

A pause for consideration. "A mistake on my part. We seemed to have a lot in common to begin with. Was she being nasty to you?"

"Is *she* one of your guests tonight?"

"No."

"If you ever bring her here again, don't expect me to cook for her. She might be nice to you on the outside, but inside she's a bitch."

"Simone will never be invited here again. I'm sorry she upset you, Dani."

"So you should be," she muttered. "No taste. No depth. You should have known better."

"Perhaps I couldn't find anyone better until you came into my life."

"Convenient. That's what it was with Simone."

"I guess you could say that."

"Well, if you think I'm another convenience..."

"No. I definitely don't think that. I doubt that anyone could think of you as a convenience, Dani. More like a force of nature."

She heard the smile in his voice and didn't know whether to be angry or mollified. "Well, so long as you've got things straight now..."

"Very straight." He came up behind her and dropped a soft kiss on her bare shoulder. "Thank you for standing up for me. I'm glad you think I've got a great body. And you'd better stop mangling those grapes if we're to have them tonight."

"Oh!" said Dani, her concentration shot to pieces by the touch of his warm lips on her skin. She jerked her hand up and turned off the tap. "If we're going to get any dinner tonight you'd better stop distracting me, Cameron McFarlane."

He sighed. "Another cold swim. Just when I thought you were warming to me. Well, I guess I'd better go do penance for my former sins so you'll forgive me enough to make me some lunch."

He left Dani smiling to herself. She couldn't help it. She wondered if he could charm birds out of trees. Then she wondered why he thought she was a force of nature. She finally decided Simone didn't matter. What had happened in Cameron's past was no concern of hers. What happened in the future was something else entirely.

Dani wasn't sure where she was going with Cameron. For better or for worse she loved him, which meant she probably would end up in bed with him. But how much that would mean to Cameron she didn't really know. Did he ever think of getting married? Having children and creating a family? Was that in his formula for life?

Dani was none the wiser when she left the kitchen to get changed for dinner. Everything was prepared as Cameron had dictated, leaving the minimum of work for her to do once the guests arrived. It was only a matter of popping a few things in the oven at the appropriate time and serving the courses she had planned. Cameron would handle all the drinks and wines.

She had spent some time during the afternoon washing and blow-drying her hair, happily aware that her wild cloud of crinkles and curls looked absolutely right for her dress. She bundled her hair up in a cap, had a quick shower, then took great care with her make-up. Oddly enough, even her freckles seemed right for the dress, as well. She didn't worry about trying to cover them up. She used green eye shadow and a vibrant orange lipstick and touched up her thick lashes with mascara.

The silk chiffon had a lovely sensuous feel as it slid over her bare breasts. Black shoestring ties at the back of the neck fastened the bodice of the dress in place. Dani did them up then fluffed out her hair and did a few twirls around the bedroom, feeling like a beautiful barefoot Gipsy as the wonderful skirt floated out around her. It was a pity she had to put shoes on at all, Dani thought, but she could hardly be a barefoot hostess.

She heard music playing the moment she stepped into the hallway. Cameron had put on a calypso disc, and the beat was infectious. Her feet itched to dance. She found Cameron in the living room and came to a heart-pumping halt as he stared at her and she stared at him. He wore all black. A black open-necked silk shirt with softly flowing sleeves. Severely tailored black trousers. He looked like a Gipsy, too, dark and dangerous and magnificent, his vivid eyes flashing blue fire.

He suddenly grinned. "Shall we dance?"

Dani laughed and twirled towards him. "Yes. Let's dance."

He caught her in his arms and led her into a wild tango. It was certainly playing with fire, but Dani didn't care. It was madly exciting and marvellous, and the desire glittering in Cameron's eyes ran like a fever through her blood. When he swept her hard against him, she revelled in the power of his body, the tensile strength that seemed to envelop her. When he swung her away from him, her body zinged with anticipation for the next time he would catch her, bending her over his arm, leading her wherever he willed.

The doorbell rang.

Which was probably just as well, Dani told herself, or things might have gotten completely out of hand. However, it was difficult to stifle a pang of regret that they had been interrupted, and she couldn't bring herself to protest Cameron's arm around her waist as he swept her with him to greet his guests in the foyer.

Two couples arrived together. The men were in their thirties, the women in their late twenties, Dani judged. Cameron introduced her to them and Dani tried her best to remember their names, reciting them over to herself, Ken and Barbara, Colin and Jill. All four of them seemed to have trouble tearing their eyes away from her, which was amazing since Cameron was standing beside her.

I really am *striking,* Dani thought exultantly, and shot a loving look at Cameron for making it possible. He hugged her closer to him as they ushered the guests into the living room, and Dani couldn't resist giving him a hug in return.

For the next ten minutes, Dani revelled in her role as hostess. Cameron poured champagne while she made small talk. Both the women admired her dress and asked where she had bought it. The men were content to simply admire her. No-one was yet interested in the tray of hors d'oeuvres, which was set on the low table between the leather lounges.

When the doorbell rang again, Cameron went to answer it. She was feeling wonderfully confident and happy, chatting away to Barbara and Jill, when Cameron ushered in his last two guests. She looked up in bright expectation of meeting another nice couple, and her smile froze on her face when she saw who was with Cameron.

Nicole!

And her current live-in.

Dani was numbly aware that Nicole's smile had frozen on her face at the sight of her, as well. Total shock between them.

CHAPTER TEN

DANI WRENCHED her eyes away from Nicole and looked at Cameron. His eyes were serious, looking at her with sombre purpose. Dani's heart performed an agitated little jig. He had something in mind, all right. But what?

Cameron smoothly carried out the introductions, and Dani could not help but admire the way Nicole recovered herself enough to acknowledge them. It helped speed Dani's recovery. She managed a fair semblance of composure when Cameron blithely informed everyone that Nicole was Dani's sister.

This raised the usual comments that they did not look at all alike, but for the first time in her life, Dani realised she was not coming off second-best in this comparison. Nicole was wearing a classic little black dress, extremely elegant and undoubtedly expensive, but tonight she was a pale moon to Dani's blazing sun. Nicole's eyes were very green as they took in Dani's dress and scanned her appearance.

Cameron guided Nicole and her present lover onto the lounge directly opposite Dani. He supplied them with glasses of champagne, then with the air of a conjurer who has performed his best trick of the evening, he settled on the armchair beside Dani and gave her a triumphant grin.

It slowly dawned on Dani that he'd had this confrontation in mind when he'd bought the dress for her. He had meant her to outshine Nicole. Perhaps he wanted to drive home to her that *she* was his choice. Not Nicole. Or any other woman.

Perhaps he had been so patient about getting her into bed because he wanted to get Nicole's lie out of the way first. Perhaps he was going to force the truth tonight. Yet a dinner party with other people present was hardly the place or time. Particularly with Nicole's lover here, as well. It would be in dreadful taste. Dani shook her head. The fact that Cameron had invited the two of them together was proof enough he hadn't slept with her sister.

Perhaps he thought this was a good peace-making gesture. One look at the barely veiled hostility in Nicole's eyes told Dani it wasn't going to work. The fat was in the fire. Nicole could hardly wait to pounce on her with bared claws.

Dani suddenly had a deeper appreciation of Cameron's insistence that she organize things so she didn't have to spend much time in the kitchen. She stayed with the guests while all the hors d'oeuvres were eaten, giving Nicole no opportunity at all to strike at her. When they went into the dining room, there was the business of being seated. Then Cameron was asking everyone's preference on wines while Dani made a discreet exit to the kitchen to bring in the first course.

Nicole was seated at the other end of the table to Dani so the congenial atmosphere was maintained while the cold cucumber soup was eaten. Cameron praised its delicate taste and kept smiling at Dani in a possessive kind of way. Stirring the pot, Dani thought, and could have kicked him, except she was placed between two of the male guests and not within striking range of Cameron.

The moment she rose to gather up the soup plates, Nicole was also on her feet, projecting sweet sisterly consideration. "I'll help you, Dani," she said.

Short of tearing plates out of her hands and making a disgraceful scene, there was nothing Dani could reasonably do to stop her. She shot a fulminating look at Cameron, who beamed a benevolent smile back at her.

The moment the kitchen door was closed behind them, Nicole opened fire. "What on earth are you thinking of, letting Cameron McFarlane parade you around like a whore?"

"Do you think of yourself as your lover's whore?" Dani retorted fiercely.

"I have a job and can afford this dress. I keep myself," Nicole snapped.

"I keep myself, too, Nicole. These clothes come with the job of being Cameron's personal chef."

"His what?"

"His personal chef. He offered me the job and I took it. I cook all his meals for him and he pays me a . . . a very large salary."

"Don't tell me you're not sharing his bed, too." Contemptuous scorn.

"I have my own bedroom. In which I sleep alone." She glared her contempt at Nicole. "People in glass houses shouldn't throw stones. And while I'm on the subject, you can tell me why you lied to me about sharing Cameron's bed yourself.''

Nicole affected a lofty look. ''It was for your own good.''

''I don't need you to make those decisions for me, Nicole.''

''Yes, you do. You never take a damned bit of notice of anything except what *you* want to do.''

The furious resentment in Nicole's voice rang bells in Dani's mind. ''You're jealous of me, aren't you, Nicole?''

Nicole's mouth tightened and her green eyes blazed with pride. ''Why should *I* be jealous of *you?*''

''I don't know,'' Dani answered truthfully. ''But you are. So why don't you spit it out, Nicole? What is it about me that gets under your skin?''

A number of expressions warred across Nicole's face, finally firming into angry decision. ''All right. I'll tell you. You do things. You don't care what anyone thinks about them. You go your own way regardless of...of anything at all. Breaking all the rules. And because you're the baby of the family, you're allowed to get away with it.''

Dani stared at her sister in bewilderment. ''What rules have I broken?''

''All of them! All the rules I had to live by. You wriggled out of them. You could get your clothes dirty. You weren't sent to bed early when you were a little kid. You were allowed to stay up until my bedtime. You could get rotten grades at school. Nothing was *expected* of you. I took the brunt of all the expectations in our family. While *you* were spoilt rotten and went your own sweet merry way."

Dani frowned as understanding started weaving through her mind. "But you get all the approval, Nicole," she reminded her sister.

"I paid for it!"

"Yes. I guess you did," Dani said slowly, sympathetically. "I'm sorry, Nicole. I didn't realise..."

"No. You never have thought about me. All the times I had the responsibility of minding you, and if you did something wrong, I got the blame for not looking after you properly. But *you* never took any damned notice of *me*."

Dani shook her head. "But you were always so prim and proper. You never wanted to have fun."

"That's all you've ever thought about. Having fun!"

"Is there something wrong with that?"

Nicole glared at her. "Of course there's something wrong with it! Why should you have fun?"

"I can tell you it hasn't been much fun for me having you always held up as the perfect model daughter," Dani retaliated. "The bright one. The beautiful one. The one who never did anything wrong. How do you think that made me feel? Dim scatty Dani with the frizzy hair and freckles."

Nicole frowned.

"I couldn't compete with you, Nicole. Just thinking about you made me feel crushed all the time because you were always better than me at everything. Don't you see?" Dani appealed. "I had to go my own way to survive as the person I am. If I tried to be like you, I was always going to be a loser, Nicole. Look at you..."

A funny little smile quirked at the corner of Nicole's mouth. "Look at you—" her eyes ran over the turbulent cloud of crinkles and curls "—even your frizzy hair looks beautiful tonight."

"But yours looks beautiful all the time, Nicole."

Her sister heaved a rueful sigh. "I guess we both have our resentments."

"We've never really talked about them. But believe me, I've been terribly jealous of you at times," Dani confessed.

"Really?" Nicole looked unsure.

This seemed almost incredible to Dani. "Dad's so proud of you. I'm the also-ran who might possibly do something good some day. But that's open to grave doubt," she added with heavy irony. "You're the shining star in our family. I think you always will be, Nicole. Whatever price you paid for being the first... you are the first."

Nicole grimaced. "Grandma always takes your side."

"Can't I have someone taking my side?"

"Why should she, when you never do anything right?"

"Maybe she likes to see me acting independently. Doing what I want instead of what everyone else wants."

"A chip off the old block," Nicole half jeered. "I can see you ending up as ornery as Grandma, Dani."

"I hope I do. I think Grandma is a great person."

Nicole looked disgruntled, as though she wanted more argument but couldn't bring anything suitable to mind. "You'll end up in Cameron McFarlane's bed, too," she finally said. "If you're not already there. He's not doing all this for nothing."

Dani was only too well aware of that. "If I do, it will be because I love him, Nicole."

The kitchen door opened and Cameron breezed in. "Anything interesting going on out here?"

"Oh, my God! The dinner!" Dani whirled to rescue the dishes she had put in the oven before the soup course.

"I'll leave you to it since you're the expert," Nicole said with a touch of the old spite.

Ingrained attitudes died hard, Dani thought, pulling on her oven gloves. Nevertheless, the spite had less acid than usual, and now all their grievances had been aired, perhaps they could be a little more sisterly to each other in future.

Nicole and Cameron exchanged false smiles as he opened the door for her exit. "Everything all right, Dani?" he asked with a look of concern.

"Fine!"

"Need a helping hand?"

"I think you've *helped* quite enough tonight," she said pointedly. "Go on back to your guests, Cameron. I'll get this served up in a minute."

"They can wait another minute," he said, his eyes twinkling with mischievous purpose as he moved towards her and swept her into his arms.

"What do you think you're doing?" Dani demanded, waving her heavily gloved hands in protest.

"It's been a long time since last Saturday night," he said, and claimed her mouth with his, effectively silencing any further protest.

Dani's mind was torn in two. This wasn't the right time. Yet he was kissing her so beautifully, so temptingly, that everything within her cried out to respond. But her hands were trapped in the stupid padded gloves, and she didn't like the helpless feeling that gave her. Cameron was in control of everything, while she... With an inward sigh Dani gave in to what he was doing to her. He was so good at it, and it *had* been a long time since Saturday night.

She completely lost track of time, place and circumstances, drugged by the intoxicating sensations Cameron aroused in her. How long the kiss went on, Dani had no idea, but it was Cameron's decision to bring it to an end, not hers. Slowly, reluctantly, their lips parted, and when she opened her eyes, she saw a blaze of intent purpose in his.

"Tonight, Dani," he murmured, and there was no mistaking what he meant. The issue of Nicole was cleared away, and Dani couldn't deny that her desire for him was as strong as his for her.

But did Cameron love her?

The question tormented Dani's mind and heart as she watched him return to the dining room. Perhaps it was all a game to him, a game he played with masterly skill to get what he wanted. The greater the challenge, the more he enjoyed it, searching out and finding the right psychological buttons to press, pacing his timing to maximum potential and impact. The dress, the dancing tonight, the intimate smiles at the table, the settlement with Nicole, the kiss . . .

Cameron McFarlane was a man who knew too much about people, how they felt and thought and acted. Maybe that was why he had refused to let her read his books. He didn't want her to know how much he knew. He wanted her responding to him exactly as he planned it, and his timetable was being brought to a close tonight.

What if it was all aimed for a chapter in his next book?

Fear clutched her heart and turmoil reigned in her mind. But she had a dinner to serve, guests who were waiting, and maybe she was confusing herself for no good reason. Perhaps Cameron did truly love her and wanted her to be happy.

She opened the oven door and smoke billowed out at her. Horror seized her for several seconds, then the need for action took over. She removed all the dishes from the oven in frantic haste, closed the door on the smoke, then raced around, throwing every window in the kitchen wide open.

Heart racing, she ran to the oven, bewildered over what had gone wrong. One look at the thermostat told her the awful truth. In her mental distraction over Nicole's presence she had inadvertently turned the temperature up far too high. *Disastrously* high!

With tears pricking her eyes, she examined the results of her ghastly mistake. The honeyed carrots Cameron had liked so much were too burnt to serve. Part of the Lamb Navarin casserole was stuck to the bottom of its dish. Dani knew that the burnt taste would have permeated the rest of it. The bain-marie had no water left, an ominous sign for the vegetable charlottes, which were to have been masterpieces of colour and taste.

Utter disaster!

So much for one of the world's leading experts!

It was too late to cook anything else. The meal had been delayed too long as it was, what with Nicole and Cameron distracting her from her work. Not that that was any excuse. This was all her fault for not keeping her mind on her job. She had no choice but to serve what she could and hope it wouldn't taste too bad.

In sheer wretched misery Dani took the warmed dinner plates from the second oven and set them out. The vegetable charlottes were stuck to the inside of their moulds. Instead of a beautiful neat mound displaying the three separated colours of white cauliflower, orange sweet potato and green spinach, she had to dig out a mash of them. They were at least edible, although horribly overcooked. What was usable of the Lamb Navarin only allowed for small portions on each plate. Dani gave herself only one spoonful, hoping no-one would notice. The burnt taste wasn't quite as bad as she anticipated, but it was there for any discerning palate. The carrots were impossible.

People would just have to fill up on bread, Dani thought miserably. They probably had already, since the main course was so long in coming. She felt as though the world was sitting heavily on her shoulders when she wheeled the traymobile into the dining room. She served everyone as fast as she could and sat down, her face burning with shame.

No-one said a word about the meal. Dani couldn't look at their faces. She *felt* the quizzical frowns. A professional chef delivering *this?* Finally Nicole made a sisterly remark.

"What did you do with this casserole, Dani? It has a funny taste."

Dani took a deep breath to ease the awful constriction in her chest. "I burnt it," she blurted. Then there was nothing to do but throw an apologetic look at everyone. "Sorry. I hope it isn't too bad."

Polite denials came thick and fast.

"Well, you can't get everything right all the time," was Nicole's consoling comment.

Nicole was in splendid spirits for the rest of the evening. *At least I gave someone pleasure,* Dani thought ruefully. And as Nicole said, not even she could ruin a fresh fruit platter.

Dani consoled herself with the continental cheesecake, which *was* up to her usual standard, but the evening was ruined as far as she was concerned. Cameron couldn't possibly want to keep her on as his personal chef when she made such a mess of things. Particularly for his guests. Although perhaps he had never cared about her cooking. Perhaps that had nothing to do with anything except as a means to an end.

Somehow she couldn't bring herself to look at him to see what he was thinking. It took all her willpower to keep up a hostess face until everyone mercifully took their leave. Cameron slid his arm around her waist as they said goodbye to the last couple, but the moment the door closed behind them, Dani whirled away from him in a fever of confused rejection.

"Dani!" Sharp and urgent.

"You can fire me!" she hurled at him, churning with too many mixed-up feelings to sort anything out.

He started striding around the other side of the fountain, obviously meaning to block her path into the living room from the foyer. "I don't want to fire you. Who cares about one messed-up meal?"

"It was your fault!" she yelled at him across the ornamental pool. She swung towards the front door, determined not to let him near her. "If Nicole hadn't been here I would've got it right. You deliberately invited her for your own ends. And then kissing me in the middle of it! It's definitely all your fault. Definitely!"

Cameron turned, determined on getting to her. "Of course, it's all my fault. You're completely exonerated of any blame. But a man's got a right to clear his name, hasn't he?"

"Not at my expense. If you'd left me alone..."

"That's the problem. I can't leave you alone."

Dani wasn't soothed by these mollifying words. It *was* his fault. And no way was he going to get her tonight! "You planned it all, didn't you?" Dani hotly accused, circling the other way. "The dress..."

"You loved the dress! You wanted to wear it!"

"Bringing Nicole here to show me off in front of her..."

"Why shouldn't I show you off? Aren't I allowed to be proud of the woman I want?"

"That wasn't why you did it!" Dani shouted, changing direction again to keep the fountain between them. "You were softening me up for the kill. It's all one big game to you. But I don't play games, and I won't play your games. Let me tell you, I don't play at making love, Cameron McFarlane, so you'd better think again."

"I was opening Nicole up like an oyster, Dani. Making her confront the woman you are and forcing her to come to terms with it. It was the best way to do it."

"You could have at least warned me!"

"You would have had your guard up and nothing would have been resolved," he argued. "There was something very wrong between you and your sister for Nicole to lie as she did. Shock tactics break down barriers. Truth comes spilling out. That's what happened, wasn't it? You got things sorted out between you, didn't you?"

"That's not the point!"

"It is the point. You said you couldn't take me home on Christmas Day because of her. Why should I let it rest there when I want to be with you?"

"It was devious . . ."

"It was obvious."

Dani kept pacing angrily, yet she was forced to concede that without Cameron as the catalyst, she and Nicole might never have seen each other's point of view. So some good had come out of it. She could no longer feel her old hostility toward Nicole. She didn't even feel jealous of her any more.

But that only proved Cameron knew too much about people. Including her. "I don't think I like you, Cameron McFarlane," she said broodingly.

"Yes, you do. I'm the man you want, Dani Halstead. If you'll only be still long enough, I'll show you how much I want you, and I'll show you how much you want me."

He was right about that, Dani thought feverishly. He could do it. "I'm not going to be forced into anything by you," she hurled at him. "I will not have a time limit put on when I go to bed with you. I'm not even sure I want to go to bed with you. In fact, I'm certain I don't. I make my own decisions, Cameron McFarlane."

"Then stop fooling around and decide! Because I'm not playing any game. I won't be played with, either." He hurled the words at her. "Make up your mind about me, Dani. Here and now!"

The challenge brought Dani to a halt. There was nothing cold or calculated about it. She could see Cameron was every bit as worked up as she was. Suddenly the whole argument seemed stupid because she did want him. He was the only man she wanted. And she was biting off her nose to spite her face.

"All right," she said, pushing aside the turmoil of fear that suddenly welled up in her. If Cameron didn't love her... well, she would soon find out.

"All right, what?" he demanded.

"I'll go to bed with you," she rushed out, sealing her fate with him once and for all.

"At last!" A triumphant grin spread across his face. Cameron, the victor!

It goaded Dani into a last-minute defiance. "But only if you can catch me."

"I've got to what?" he asked incredulously.

"Catch me," Dani said with satisfaction. Cameron needn't start thinking he could have everything his way. She kicked off her shoes, ready to dodge away from him.

He laughed at her, a wild exultant laughter. "I'll catch you." And there was real determination in his voice.

A glorious madness possessed Dani as they faced each other across the ornamental pool, Cameron stalking her like a fever-mad hunter, Dani teasing him over which way she would go next. The fear of the unknown was forgotten in the excitement of the contest.

"I'll get you, Dani Halstead. If it's the last thing I ever do, I'll get you," he declared. "If I have to leap over tall buildings, go faster than a speeding bullet, plunge through boiling rapids..."

He came straight at her, right through the water, shoes and all, slipping on the mossy rocks, barking his shins against the sculptured driftwood, splashing spray everywhere. He gave a yelp of pain, but nothing was going to diminish his ardour or determination.

"Oh, dear!" said Dani. "You've hurt yourself."

He roared like a banshee possessed when he fell over part of the fountain, but he was on his feet again in an instant, coming after her with deadly intent. He made a decisive lunge that Dani evaded.

"I didn't mean you to get hurt, Cameron," she cried, then was off down the hallway to the bedroom wing.

The waiting game was over. She was ready to be caught, but didn't know what Cameron would do once he did catch her. She headed for the master bedroom. Fortunately the door was open and she made a running dive onto Cameron's king-size bed, laughing and shrieking when Cameron dived after her.

"You're wet! You're wet! You'll ruin my beautiful dress!"

She tumbled off the other side of the bed in a wild froth of silk chiffon. He leapt up and guarded the door against her escaping. He pointed an accusing finger at her.

"You...you are a terrible woman, Dani Halstead."

"Dear Cameron," she said meekly, backing away from him as he advanced on her.

"Nothing on heaven or earth is going to stop me from doing all I've wanted to do since I first met you." He started unbuttoning his shirt.

Dani was half-mesmerised by the action. "I thought you enjoyed all that time with me, Cameron," she protested. Although he had never made any secret of what he wanted, Dani desperately wanted a great deal more from him.

"I did. I surely did," he acknowledged, "but this is the moment I've been waiting for." His shirt hit the floor. He ripped off his wet shoes and socks and started undoing his trousers.

Sheer panic welled up inside her at the thought of what was to be revealed in the next few seconds. "Go towel yourself dry, Cameron."

"No." He was pulling his trousers down.

"Why not?" she asked quickly.

"I haven't got time."

"Yes, you have," she shrieked and leapt onto the bed, bounding across it to the other side.

He was waiting for her at the door, his trousers held up by his hands. "Not this again," he groaned.

"If I get you a towel from your bathroom..."

"Okay."

"No tricks."

"Scout's honour."

He was stark naked when she returned. Dani threw him the towel as quickly as she could. He rubbed himself briskly.

"If you want to keep that dress intact, Dani, you'd better take it off now," he warned, his eyes glittering frustration at the delay. No more, they said. Not one damned thing more was going to stop him or get in his way!

This is it, Dani thought. Crunch time. Will he still want me when this is over? Will he think I'm still desirable and sexy and perfect? Will he kiss me tenderly afterwards, and say I love you?

While she had exulted in the thrilling power of making him chase her, she had inadvertently aroused Cameron to fever pitch, and he didn't know she was a virgin, didn't know she had played a childish game because it had helped to lighten what was a frightening moment for her.

Her hands shook as she fumbled with the ties at the back of her neck. They finally fell apart, yet she couldn't bring herself to draw her bodice down. She had never been naked in front of a man before.

Cameron hurled the towel towards the bathroom door. Dani couldn't help staring at him. There was an awesome beauty in his aroused manhood that somehow matched the rest of his physique.

"Dani?"

The soft call of her name wrenched her gaze up to his. Dani didn't know it, but her eyes were swimming with vulnerability, wanting, needing him to show her she was more than a means of satisfying his desire.

"You're embarrassed?" he asked quietly.

"Yes." The word was barely audible. Her heart seemed to be in her mouth. She swallowed hard and finally found voice. "Love me gently, Cameron," she pleaded huskily. "Love me slowly."

"It will be whatever you want, Dani," he promised her, and she saw the deep caring in his eyes, the desire to please her rather than the need to possess, and fear melted into anticipation as, with confident assurance, he closed the last distance that separated them.

CHAPTER ELEVEN

CAMERON TOOK the top of her bodice from Dani's hands and peeled it down her arms, slowly uncovering her breasts, leaving them naked to his view and his touch. Yet his eyes did not leave hers, nor did he touch her, except to lift her hands to his shoulders.

Dani was caught in a thrall of anticipation, every cell in her body yearning to join with his, to feel his flesh against her own. Simply knowing that it was imminent and inevitable was an exquisite feeling in itself.

Cameron's hands moved to her waist. He slid the dress down over her hips, gathering her panties on the way. Her legs felt like jelly but she managed to step clear of her clothes. Her thighs quivered uncontrollably under Cameron's caress as he returned his hands to her waist. His fingers splayed downwards, gently pressuring her towards him.

Dani instinctively arched back, revelling in the first electric contact of stomach and thighs, meeting and savouring the strength of his maleness while reserving the excitement of feeling the soft fullness of her naked breasts press into the firm smooth muscles of his chest. She curled her hands around his shoulders and swayed forward, brushing the bare tips of them against him.

Cameron sucked in a deep breath, seemingly expanding his chest to reach out to her, wanting to feel more, yet wanting the delicious teasing as much as she did. She could see it in the glitter of his eyes, sense it in the expectant tautness of his body. It was as though they had waited all their lives for this moment and there was no need to hurry, only an intense hunger for every possible nuance of feeling they could generate between them.

Dani lifted herself on tiptoe and Cameron supported her, curving his hands around the soft cheeks of her bottom as she moved in a graceful rhythm, caressing him with her breasts.

"Dani..." It was a groan of delight and need, and Dani felt a fierce and primitive exultation in the urgent hardness that pressed against her stomach.

Cameron gathered her closer, crushing her softness to him, winding a hand through her hair, tilting her head back for him to find her mouth with his. It was a wildly passionate kiss, long and deep and avid for all they could give each other... a beautiful madness of caring and needing and wanting and feeling. His hands cupped her face as he rained kisses all over it. He wrapped his arms around her and hugged her tightly to him as he swept his mouth over her hair, hot, feverish, yearning. He sent his tongue delving into her ear, erotically sensual and exciting. Dani found intense pleasure in tasting his flesh wherever her mouth led her. Her hands skimmed over his body in loving discovery. She pressed herself closer and closer, hugging him in an ecstasy of possession ... her man, so wonderfully, gloriously right for her in every way.

Cameron swept her off her feet and cradled her in his arms, and Dani automatically wound her arms around his neck to hold on. He laughed down at her, a ripple of wild exhilarating joy and deep male triumph.

"I didn't know there was a caveman inside me, Dani. But there is. There most definitely is," he declared as he set her down on the bed and stretched out beside her. His lips moved softly over her lips as he murmured, "But more than anything I want this to feel right for both of us."

And he kissed her with exquisite tenderness while Dani's mind was blissfully echoing his words. She couldn't help herself. Her hands moved instinctively to stroke his shoulders and trace the interplay of the strong muscles on his back. Cameron did not protest. He trailed warm kisses down her throat and circled her breasts with feather-light fingertips. Then he kissed them with such beautiful gentle loving that Dani wanted it to go on and on forever. She barely noticed him gradually increasing the pressure of his mouth, but she was excitingly aware of changes starting inside her, a sweet melting that spread right down her thighs and aroused a quivery sense of anticipation.

Dani floated off into a limbless, boneless world of sensations. She felt as though she were turning into warm liquid. Cameron's caresses and kisses bathed her whole body in streams of pleasure. Her legs instinctively wrapped around him, hugging this wonderful man to her, *her* man. Her body lifted and fell, ululating with the ecstatic rhythm of the waves flowing through her.

Her legs slid down the hard muscular power of his thighs as Cameron prepared to enter her. His blue eyes blazed with a feverish possessiveness. Dani felt the same way. She reached out, and her touch was enough to send his stomach muscles into rippling spasms. He cried out her name, then lowered himself to finally join his body to hers.

The revelation of that moment was like a sunburst through Dani's mind and body. The unbelievable fulfilment of feeling him move inside her, of feeling herself closing around him, of possessing him, deeper and deeper... Oh, yes, Dani cried somewhere in her head. Yes, yes, yes. The words seemed to reverberate through her whole body, an exultation, a knowledge as deep and primitive as any knowledge.

She knew the way to respond to this coming together instinctively, moving her body to the strong beat of his, as graceful as a dance, swinging this way and that, a subtle rolling, closing, sliding, never quite apart, the power and the glory of it sweeping them on and on.

There was the sensation of rushing towards some stormy peak, then Dani felt herself go over the top, out of control. Her thighs were shaking uncontrollably, and there was a moment of release, of gratification, of scintillating satisfaction. Her mind seemed to split in two, to separate her from the real world, and her body floated away on a wave of euphoria.

Cameron enfolded her in his arms and carried her with him as he rolled onto his side. Dani felt his heart pounding madly and his breath rasp through her hair. His flesh was slicked with sweat, but he felt so good to Dani that she hugged him with all the love she felt for him.

She lay still, unable to do otherwise, soaking up peace, contentment and fulfilment. She sensed it spreading through him, too, tension draining away, heartbeat slowing. Eventually he moved a hand, trailing it through her long turbulent hair, circling it around her back. She heard him take a deep breath, but even so, his voice was not at full strength when he spoke.

"Dani..." Somehow he injected her name with all the magic of the world.

She smiled and grazed her lips across the base of his throat, knowing that it had been as good for him as it had been for her.

"Did I hurt you?" he asked tenderly.

"No. You were wonderful," she whispered, her heart too full to find much voice.

"So were you. Unbelievably wonderful." His arm tightened around her and he swept warm kisses over her hair. "You are one very special woman, Dani. Remind me to send Mrs. B a huge Christmas hamper for sending you to me. That was my lucky day."

Mine, too, Dani thought. Maybe her luck was changing for the better. Of course, the best possible stroke of luck would be if Cameron loved her enough to want her with him always. To want marriage and children and grandchildren and all the things that would make their life together really meaningful.

"What do you want, Dani?"

She didn't stop to think he might be asking her what she wanted for Christmas. She answered straight from her heart.

"Marriage. I want you to marry me."

She felt his shock. He went unnaturally still, not even breathing. Dani had an awful feeling that what they had just shared *was* the beginning of the end, and while she could not regret the experience of loving, her heart suddenly went heavy.

Then Cameron slowly exhaled a long breath. "I admire your directness, Dani," he said. "I really do. But..."

With a swift lithe movement, he rolled her onto her back and leaned over her, his eyes blazing straight into hers.

"I will not allow you to take my male prerogatives away from me," he stated emphatically. "I'll decide if I want to marry you. And I'll do the asking. Is that clear?"

"Does that mean no?"

"I didn't say that."

"I'm sorry. I shouldn't have said what I did. I felt so happy..."

"I want you to be happy."

"Forgive me?"

"As long as you never say it again."

"I promise." Cameron was not saying an outright no. Dani smiled at him, her eyes shining with happy hope. "I'm sorry, Cameron. I didn't mean to make your decision for you. Or influence you."

He gave her a stern look. "I'm the man. You're the woman. That's the way it stays. I don't care how screwed up the rest of the world is, I'm running my life as I see fit. And no woman, absolutely no woman, tells me when I get married."

"Yes, Cameron," she said meekly. "I understand that perfectly. I like to run my life as I see fit, too. And I most definitely don't want a man who doesn't know his own mind."

He looked suspiciously at her. "Why do I have a feeling there's a catch in that?"

"Well, it's like you wanting me to come to bed with you, Cameron," she explained as sweetly as she could. "There comes a time when you have to decide. It won't stay open-ended forever. That's not fair. You do have to make up your mind."

His mouth quirked. "You want to walk away from me, Dani?"

"No. I was wondering if you were going to walk away from me. Or fly, as the case may be. You said you were flying to the U.S. on Boxing Day."

"I've postponed the trip."

"Oh!"

"Indefinitely."

"Oh!"

"I may never go."

"Oh?"

"I find myself otherwise occupied."

"With what?"

"You."

"Well," said Dani, thinking it was a good idea to keep him very occupied. Cameron may not have made up his mind about marrying her, but at present he was definitely obsessed. "Did you hurt yourself, uh, very much when you were chasing me?"

"Terribly," he said sternly. "For which I will need a great deal of tender loving care."

"I'm not as good as Grandma, yet," she said, stroking her fingers lightly down his abdomen. "She has healing hands. But I can practise on you, Cameron, and maybe you'll feel better."

Her feather touch found some erotic spots under his hipbones, and Cameron responded very strongly. "Keep that up and you'll have your grandmother beaten, hands down," he rasped.

"Maybe if I..."

"Dani..." It was a half-strangled sound.

Cameron didn't need any more healing. He proceeded to show Dani how occupied he could be with her. It took him most of the night. When he woke her the next day after a long languorous sleep, he aroused her to intensely pleasurable consciousness and continued on from where he had left off, demonstrating a dedication to being obsessively occupied for a long time.

CHAPTER TWELVE

CHRISTMAS DAY!

Dani wore a grin a mile wide as she and Cameron set off for her parents' home. This was what she had wanted from her first meeting with Cameron, but she had only envisaged a superficial charade at the time. Now it was the real thing. Cameron McFarlane *was* her man, to all intents and purposes.

Although he hadn't yet come to marriage, Dani felt he might be coming close. He certainly showed no signs of wanting to be apart from her. In fact, it seemed that he really couldn't leave her alone. Or didn't want to. He even drove with one hand so that he could hold hers, his fingers occasionally stroking a possessive caress.

There were other good signs for the future that made Dani feel hopeful. As well as buying Mrs. B a huge hamper, Cameron had bought all her family Christmas presents. That, to Dani, was a clear indication that he wanted to be part of her family. Which, she was sure, would be good for him since he didn't have a family of his own. She did caution herself that Cameron was generous by nature, but that didn't stop her from hoping.

Besides, her luck was changing. It had to be. All three of her disasters had turned into triumphs. She had the best job in the world cooking for Cameron. Mrs. B was in seventh heaven with her Henry. And today was going to be the best Christmas Day ever. It was already the best with Cameron beside her, looking devastatingly handsome in white jeans and a navy blue sports shirt.

Dani's parents lived at Wamberal on the Central Coast, about an hour's journey north of Sydney. Their house was situated on a hill and overlooked the beaches that stretched around the coast as far as the eye could see. It was a good solid comfortable home, nothing luxurious like Cameron's, but the view was lovely, and the veranda overlooking it was wide and spacious. This was where her parents did all their summer relaxing and entertaining. They were seated out there with Grandma when Dani and Cameron pulled up in the driveway.

Although Dani had informed her mother she was bringing Cameron home with her, she had thought it wiser not to spell out their actual relationship. No point in stirring up worries when there might not be any worries at all, she argued to herself. Of course, Nicole could be the fly in the ointment if she had a mind to be, but Dani had decided to give her elder sister the benefit of the doubt. Perhaps they could live and let live this Christmas. Besides, surely Nicole would think twice about saying anything nasty in front of Cameron.

When she and Cameron alighted from the car, Dani saw her mother's eyes open wide and her father's eyebrows lift in startled surprise. Her grandmother simply smiled. Greetings were called out, introductions made, and her father came down to shake Cameron's hand and help carry up the Christmas parcels.

The next half-hour was sheer bliss for Dani. Her parents were completely bowled over by Cameron, who sat holding her hand and throwing her smiles that could only be read as besotted devotion. Which made Dani stand extremely tall in her parents' eyes. They didn't ask one question about her career. Grandma watched, nodding her head occasionally.

The old familiar tension hit Dani when Nicole arrived with her man. She couldn't help worrying whether her sister would be content to let sleeping dogs lie. Yet, much to Dani's pleasant surprise and relief, Nicole seemed happy to accept Cameron's presence and didn't even make a sly dig to Dani about it. In fact, as they sat drinking long glasses of Christmas punch, Nicole actually smiled at her, to which Dani swiftly responded, thinking that her sister had somehow become imbued with real Christmas spirit.

She was even more startled when Nicole engineered a private conversation with her and started it with what seemed to be a sincere apology. "I'm sorry for saying what I did about Cameron, Dani. If you really have something going together..."

"Nicole..." Dani hesitated, but it was a question she felt she had to ask. "Was it because you wanted Cameron for yourself?"

Slowly she shook her head. "Not really. I fancied him. What woman wouldn't? But Barry..."

The look Nicole gave her man sent a flood of relief through Dani.

"We're thinking of getting married."

If only Cameron would think of getting married, Dani thought, but she swiftly stifled the little stab of envy. It was time for her to be generous, too. "How wonderful for you, Nicole."

"Yes, it is." Nicole gave an ironic smile. "Barry doesn't mind about the rules I've broken. It was a kind of rebellion...sleeping with anyone I fancied. But that's not what I want. It was stupid. I ended up not liking myself very much."

"I'm sorry you felt like that," Dani said softly.

Nicole looked at her curiously. "You feel good about yourself, don't you, Dani? You always projected that."

Dani grimaced. "Not always. Two weeks ago I felt like a complete failure, wondering how I was going to face up to the family on Christmas Day. I didn't have a job. My prospects were pretty grim..."

"But now you have Cameron?"

"Yes. Now I have Cameron." More or less, she thought.

"I hope, truly hope you'll be happy with him. Now that I'm happy I want everyone in the world to be happy."

There could be no doubting her sister's sincerity. A dark weight lifted from Dani's heart. She gave her sister a brilliant smile. "Thanks, Nicole. I wish you every happiness, too."

Nicole turned back to Barry, and Dani turned her smile to Cameron, who had made this new harmony with her sister possible. His eyes sparkled knowingly at her, and Dani felt truly grateful that he was so good at psychology. She made up her mind to read all his books now that he could have no objection.

He was talking to Grandma, and Dani was delighted to see that they had established a rapport in no time flat. The liking between them was obviously genuine. Dani could tell by the warmth in Cameron's eyes and the twinkling smiles Grandma kept giving him. Of course, Cameron could charm birds out of trees when he had a mind to, but Grandma was not one to be taken in by superficial charm. She really liked him. No doubt about that.

Eventually Dani's parents declared it was time for the gifts to be opened and they were all ushered into the lounge, where the Christmas tree took pride of place. Dani manoeuvred a private little chat with Grandma on the way.

"Well, now you've met him, Grandma."

"Yes, dear."

"What do you think?"

"I think he has a lot of Irish in him."

"Grandma, you couldn't get a more Scottish name than Cameron McFarlane."

"Gaelic blood. It's all the same."

"Do you think he's like Grandpa?" Dani asked.

Grandma nodded wisely. "He's certainly a man who knows his own mind and fights for what he wants."

Which was fairly spot on, Dani thought appreciatively.

"I think lamb roast would be best," Grandma mused.

Dani looked her bewilderment. "What about lamb roast?"

"Men like him are plain eaters. Plain eaters like lamb roast. He is a plain eater, isn't he?"

"Well, more or less." Dani had been doing her best to teach him better.

"Don't cook fancy," Grandma advised. "He'll say he likes it to please you, but inwardly he'll get indigestion. Give him lamb roast. I always found your grandfather very amenable to any suggestion after I fed him lamb roast."

"Right!" said Dani. "I've got it. Lamb roast. Thank you, Grandma."

The brown eyes twinkled at her and Dani gave her a quick hug. She felt very happy.

Dani's father put an end to any further conversation. "Dani, since you're wearing red and white, you can be Santa Claus this year and give out the presents from under the tree," he announced, beaming more approval at her than he had ever done before.

Cameron grinned at her as he settled on the two-seater sofa with Grandma. "Show some Christmas spirit, Dani," he teased.

She laughed and fossicked through the presents to find one for her mother first. "Happy Christmas, Mum," she said as she handed it to her.

"It is indeed, Dani," she said with a happy smile.

Everyone was happy. Nicole even managed to look delighted with the Lancôme soap. Dani had felt a bit mean about that gift, so she had wrapped the soap in a pair of French lace knickers, which brought a real sparkle to Nicole's eyes, particularly when she looked at Barry.

Cameron laughed delightedly over the collection of things Dani had bought him—a ruler for drawing a straight line, a coffee mug with Good Morning printed on it, a bath towel marked His, a man's kitchen apron depicting a burning barbecue, and a glass-enclosed tableau of a tropical fountain which, when shaken, looked as though spray was going everywhere. Inside it was a little man who tumbled around in the splashing droplets.

Christmas wrapping paper was strewn all over the floor by the time Dani came to the last present. She had deliberately left Cameron's gift to her to the end although she was dying to open it to see what he'd selected for her. It was a rectangular shape, the size of a ladies' purse.

She was conscious of him watching her as she tore off the wrapping, so she threw him a special smile to let him know that whatever it was she would love it. Inside was a velvet box, the kind that would hold an expensive necklace.

Dani took a deep breath, only too aware that Cameron thought nothing of spending a fortune on her. She hoped he hadn't gone terribly wild this time. She unlatched the lid and lifted it up, expecting almost anything except what was there.

In the centre of a groove running across the black velvet was a magnificent solitaire diamond ring. Lying behind it was a card on which Cameron had written, "Will you marry me?"

Her gaze flew up to his—beautiful blue eyes beaming love and commitment straight into her heart. Dani felt too choked with emotion to speak. She got to her feet and carried the box over to him, all the love she felt for him in her eyes. She gave him the box, then held out her left hand for him to put the ring on her finger.

"Say yes," he prompted, his eyes glittering intense and relentless purpose.

"Yes," she whispered.

He pulled her onto his lap and nestled her in the crook of one arm, holding her possessively while he opened the box. He slid the fabulous diamond ring onto the third finger of her left hand with slow deliberate ceremony.

"Marriage," he said decisively. "So now you're well and truly caught."

"Yes," she agreed, finally managing to find her voice. "You caught me, Cameron."

"And there's no getting away."

"Absolutely none."

"Divorce is out."

"Unthinkable."

"Children."

"Yes, children."

"And grandchildren."

"Only if you're capable, dear Cameron."

"I'm *very* capable," he asserted strongly. Then he looked around the assembled family, who were all stunned into silence. "That's it. Dani and I are getting married."

It was definitely the best Christmas Day ever—an impossible dream come true!

When they went to bed together that night, Cameron told Dani again and again how much he loved her. Dani had no compunction whatsoever in impressing on Cameron how much she loved him, too.

A VERY LONG, LONG TIME later, after many things had happened—and this is absolutely true—Dani and Cameron retired to a hobby farm. Dani had her chickens and her fruit trees and her herb and vegetable garden. Cameron took a lively interest in breeding cashmere goats for their wool and Australian silky terriers for the fun of it. It was a good life, full of interesting things happening and sweetened with the contentment of sharing everything together.

Occasionally their children tried to tell them they were getting too old for this kind of life, but Dani and Cameron were determined to live how they wanted to live. After all, that was what they had been doing together all their lives, and they had every right to be stubborn and ornery about it.

Grandchildren came to them for their school holidays, and that was always a lot of fun. Sometimes they whispered together about the mysterious way Grandma knew so much about what they did. They didn't really believe that the birds told her everything. They finally figured out she had some kind of sixth sense that let her know things that even Grandpa didn't know.

Grandma was also wonderful at baking cakes and cookies. They all reckoned she was so good that she could have been a professional cook if she'd wanted to be. Her roast lamb dinners were the best! And her homemade pea and ham soup, which was Grandpa's favourite, was out of this world. The kitchen was always full of delicious smells.

Though whenever anyone got hurt or sick, Grandma was good at that, too. She had soft soothing hands that seemed to comfort all the way inside you. You definitely went to Grandma if you got wounded.

She also had a special part in her brain for wise old sayings. How she knew so many of them was another mystery. She must have been storing them up in her memory ever since she was born. Press a button and out one would come.

It was funny, though, how they seemed to fit whatever was going on. Her fairy stories were like that, too. All the grandchildren agreed it was positively uncanny the way Grandma hit right at the heart of things. She really knew everything.

When anyone wanted some serious advice, the farm was undoubtedly the best place to go. When Danielle McFarlane was fifteen she needed serious advice. Very serious advice. She arrived at the farm on an impromptu visit.

All the grandchildren thought Grandma loved them best, but this one, who had been named after her, was closest to Grandma's heart. Young Dani smiled and chatted, but underneath the surface she was troubled. A very difficult problem weighed on her mind.

Grandpa and Grandma exchanged a knowing look, part of the intimacy that had grown between them over the years. Words weren't necessary between them at times like these. Grandpa excused himself, saying he had to go and see his dogs. Grandma waited for young Dani to tell her the problem that had brought her out of her way today.

"I want to ask you something, Grandma."

"Yes, dear?" Dani threaded her needle, picked up her latest tapestry, then looked at her grand-daughter, who was frowning heavily.

"It's about a boy. Well, not really a boy. He's sixteen. All the girls drool over him because he's so good-looking. I know I'm not the prettiest girl in the school but he seems to like me . . ."

Dani glanced out the kitchen window. Cameron was still so upright and tall, walking towards the far fence, one of their dogs prancing at his heels. He was almost eighty years old, but he was a fine figure of a man. White-haired, but his eyes were as blue as they ever were, and they hadn't lost their sparkling kindness, nor their wickedness. What a wonderful life they'd had! All these years . . . and the love they shared was a continual celebration of their life together.

But she mustn't think of that now. She had to help young Dani. She gave her grand-daughter an encouraging smile and went back to her stitching. Bit by bit the problem emerged, and Dani was transported back almost fifty years. When it was time for her to speak, she knew exactly what to say.

"Beauty," she said, "is in the eye of the beholder."

She knew Dani would be disappointed in that answer.

"Well, Grandma, I suppose I'd better be on my way..."

"Before you go, Dani, I think I have to tell you a story. It's a fairy story. But for all it's a fairy story, it's true enough. It happened a long, long time ago. See what you make of it."

She paused, remembering all her own feelings, the beginning of her love for Cameron, his for her. But her grand-daughter was waiting to hear the story, to learn, if she could.

"Once upon a time, there was a young girl..."

As CAMERON DROVE his grand-daughter to the railway station, he grew conscious of young Dani shooting curious glances at him, as though she was appraising him in a new light.

"Something wrong, Dani?" he asked.

"No, Grandpa. Nothing wrong," she denied, and gave him a funny little smile. It held both satisfaction and bemusement. Then she said, "But I would like to know..."

"Know what?"

"Did Grandma really find black lace knickers in your bed when she first met you?"

When Cameron returned to the farm, he found his wife standing dreamily in front of the kitchen window. "Did you have a good day today?" he asked, giving her a hug, their closeness and their love reflected in his twinkling blue eyes.

Since the day they married, Cameron insisted that every woman who was loved should be given three hugs a day. He said it was to show her that no matter what happened, they would always be together. Dani never raised any question about this, but she suspected it had a bit to do with reassuring a man that his woman was well and truly caught.

"Oh, yes, dear," she said. "I had another wonderful day. Everything turned out as it should."

Her mind supplied another thought—all's well that ends well—but she didn't need to voice that to Cameron. His smile said it for her. And when she smiled back he saw no signs of age at all. He saw only the girl who had once come into his bedroom and woke him up to what life could be like . . . if he could catch her and keep her with him.

He still had her!

Where do you find hot Texas nights, smooth Texas charm and dangerously sexy cowboys?

COWBOYS AND CABERNET

Raise a glass—Texas style!

Tyler McKinney is out to prove a Texas ranch is the perfect place for a vineyard. Vintner Ruth Holden thinks Tyler is too stubborn, too impatient, too... Texas. And far too difficult to resist!

CRYSTAL CREEK reverberates with the exciting rhythm of Texas. Each story features the rugged individuals who live and love in the Lone Star State. And each one ends with the same invitation...

Y'ALL COME BACK... REAL SOON!

Don't miss *COWBOYS AND CABERNET* by Margot Dalton. Available in April wherever Harlequin books are sold.

HARLEQUIN ✦ PRESENTS®

A Year DOWN UNDER

In 1993, Harlequin Presents celebrates the land down under. In April, let us take you to Queensland, Australia, in A DANGEROUS LOVER by Lindsay Armstrong, Harlequin Presents #1546.

Verity Wood usually manages her temperamental boss, Brad Morris, with a fair amount of success. At least she *had* until Brad decides to change the rules of their relationship. But Verity's a widow with a small child—the last thing she needs, or wants, is a dangerous lover!

Share the adventure—and the romance—
of A Year Down Under!

Available this month in
A YEAR DOWN UNDER

THE GOLDEN MASK
by Robyn Donald
Harlequin Presents #1537
Wherever Harlequin books are sold.   YDU-M